THE
CAPTAIN'S
SPELL

A NOVELLA & THREE STORIES

JASON GRUNSPAN

The story The Company of Crows first appeared in Prime Number Magazine.

The story, all names, characters, and incidents portrayed in this production are fictitious. No identification with actual persons (living or deceased), places, buildings, and products is intended or should be inferred.

Author inquiries should be sent to hairybearpublishing@gmail.com

eBook ISBN: 979-8-218-34325-5
Paperback ISBN: 979-8-218-34324-8
Hardcover ISBN: 979-8-218-34518-1

1. Fiction/ Historical 2. Fiction/ Sea Stories
3. Fiction/ Magical Realism 4. Fiction/ Short Stories

Cover Illustration by Kaitlynn Jolley

Thanks to Eric Grunspan for his editorial feedback

First edition 2023

Table of Contents

Table of Contents

To the memory of Ruth Grunspan—thanks mom

THE CAPTAIN'S SPELL

Chapter 1

I am the ship clown, like a jester from the olden days, meant to entertain and provide reprieve from the cruel relentless sea. I understand it's one of the reasons he brought me aboard as the captain does nothing by chance. And perhaps it's why he now confides in me, calling me to his quarters well after the red sun has melted into the distant horizon, so dark that I place my hand on the steel rail which traces the outer deck, to keep my bearings.

Surely he didn't accept me aboard because of my experience. The only boat I'd ever been on was old man Weaver's fishing skiff. By then, the old boy was half blind and deaf in one ear, and he'd paid me to help navigate and keep from crashing into oncoming vessels. Wasn't because of my great physical prowess either, as there are bigger, stronger men.

Apparently the captain had seen me in port plucking my guitar on street corners for change, because when he hired me aboard he told me to bring my guitar and good humor—that at some point they'd be as much needed as food, whiskey and fair weather.

As I make my way along the deck breathing the salted sea air, the waves wash against the hull with rhythmic force and the ship's old bones creak and moan. By habit I look about for the light of another vessel but there's only the dark curtain of night.

Kronen is on watch, standing atop the forecastle at the edge of the bow, his form illuminated by a frail yellow light. Hearing my steps, he turns and I nod up at him but he doesn't return the greeting. He is the captain's right hand, his henchman and sycophant; a slithering snake of a man none of the crew trusts. He scowls past me into the dark abyss, knowing I'm going to see the captain (Where else could I be going?) I've become a threat to his status as the captain's chief confidant, and to Kronen nothing could be more unsettling. I can almost hear his muttered curses and know he's scheming a way to turn the tables, or more likely, waiting for a chance to send me overboard.

I pull open a hatch and cautiously make my way down narrow steps into the ships belly, until I'm facing an oval shaped door. The shift in atmosphere is sharp and sudden as the sea's enormity—the ferocity of its elements—is temporarily placed at bay, giving an illusion of security. I still hear the wind but its howl is a distant whine, almost soothing. I knock three times and a minute passes.

"Who is it?"

"Dent, sir."

The captain's voice startles me; I did not hear any steps approaching. He unlocks the latch and I follow him into his quarters. He sits down in a burgundy velvet armchair made to look like a throne with its over-sized back and armrests inlaid with colorful stones. Seated atop a dresser, I see the old raggedy doll he calls, "Sally" and hanging on the wall behind him, a tribal mask carved from wood with holes cut out in the nose, mouth, and eyes. On the other side of the cabin next to his bed and a quaint colonial style nightstand, is a desk with nautical charts, maps, a few books, and several more indigenous wood carvings. Our captain, I think, isn't the kind of man for whom modest, practical furnishings will suffice. This is my first time in his cabin and I'm struck by the size of it. It makes mine and the rest of the crew's berthing compartments seem like cages, and I can't but help feel envious. He motions for me to sit in a little wicker chair, facing him across a table. I squirm uncomfortably in the chair like a schoolboy summoned to the headmaster's office and again, I'm certain this is by design.

For a moment he sits quietly lost in thought, running his fingers through his beard as though stroking a cat. "Hold on a second," he says, remembering something, stands, walks to a shelf, grabs a bottle of whiskey and two glasses and places them on the table. He fills the glasses.

"Thank you for interrupting your evening plans to meet with me," he says with such pious sincerity, I can't decide if he's serious or not.

"That's quite okay, Captain, I can resume picking my nose once we're done," I say, hoping to lighten the mood. He cracks a smile, acknowledging the joke, but fails to unleash the booming, room filling laugh which seems to originate in the depths of his being.

"To every rowboat, raft, and battered oar, to all the sailors who've come before," he says, raising his glass and downing the whiskey. I follow suit, put the glass on the table and wipe my mouth with my sleeve.

"There's nothing more dangerous aboard a ship than the fraying of loyalty," he says, his tone suddenly somber. "The successful completion of our mission, our very survival, demands that my authority be acknowledged without question, my orders heeded and obeyed. Once the job is done the men can do as they like. If I greet them ashore, and they spit and curse my name, so be it. But aboard this vessel I am their captain, their father, their God-king, and need to be treated as such."

"Unfortunately, the men aren't a very religious group, Captain. And most wouldn't know their fathers if they bumped into them on the street."

"You know what I mean, and besides, it's all the more reason for them to direct their loyalty toward me."

If any acts of disloyalty have been committed, I'm not aware. I am of course aware of the quiet grumblings and speculation concerning the captain and his oddities: the fact that we've been at sea nearly a month (I believe it's nearly a month, as the days blend together in a way that makes the tracking of time difficult) and no one has seen him eat as much as a crumb, his eerie habit of appearing suddenly without a sound or indication of any kind that he was approaching, the sense you got in his presence that he wasn't what he appeared to be, or much more than he appeared to be, or not really there at all, the choosing of Kronen as his first mate.

"Has there been an incident of disloyalty?" I ask, and he stares at me with such singular, steely eyed focus that my hands tremble.

After a moment, I realize he's not staring at, but through me, such that I question whether I'm actually there. To quell my uncertainty, I grab the sides of my chair and acknowledge the aftertaste of the whiskey still burning in my nose and throat. What kind of power does this man possess, that a look from him brings me to question my very existence?

"No particular incident," he says, relaxing his gaze. "More a mood, a general attitude. I see the looks of the men, hear their whispers and discontented muttering. If not nipped in the bud it'll fester and spread like a contagious virus, taking the ship down with it.

"I'm asking that you keep your eyes and ears open, reporting back to me any situations that could be deemed a threat to the ship's safety and success."

"What kind of— "

"You're an intelligent mate, certainly smarter than this lot of inbred mongrels who've finagled their way onto my ship. I'll let you be the judge of what qualifies as report worthy."

Wasn't it he who hired them aboard? Before I can ask, he continues.

"You're attuned to the thinking and deliberations of the crew, at least as far as they're capable of such. They trust you. It's crucial you not disclose to anyone what we've discussed, or even that we've met."

Having said his peace, he lights a pipe filled to the brim with his favored cherry tobacco and leans back with it in his mouth, projecting an expression of blissful satisfaction. In his state of repose, I take a moment to consider him. His face is a compilation of contradictions and incongruent parts. It's as if someone visited a junkyard of facial features and welded together whatever they could find. The nose is long and thin, the face round and red with a pudginess in the cheeks. The chin, now hidden beneath the weeds of a brown beard, flecked with white, juts out like a crag of rock from the side of a hill. Perhaps it's because of these incongruities that each time I see him it's as though for the first time. And I'm not sure if it's the low lighting, but I swear his skin has taken on a grayish pallor not previously there.

Then there are the eyes. One green and one blue, the lids obscuring the upper portion of the irises, casting a sleepy hypnotic power over whoever holds their gaze. Having once measured you, they take you in their grip, tightening like a vice until you find yourself fighting to break free of a trance.

"What about Kronen?"

"What about him?" he says, taking another puff.

"He's on watch; he saw me going to your quarters."

"I'll handle Kronen, he's the least of my concerns right now," he says, almost before I've gotten the sentence out of my mouth. Doubts and misgivings are an affront to a man of such self-assurance, and I squirm again in my chair, understanding that I've offended him after he'd thought well enough of me to entrust me with his plans. I know his talk of being a God-king and father to the crew is self-inflated absurdity, and yet, I hold him—if not in reverence, then—with a kind of awe, and hate to disappoint him.

"Very good then, Captain," I say, nodding, and rising to my feet.

"Dent," he says, just before I reach the door. I stop and turn; he's placed the pipe to the side and leans forward in his burgundy throne. "Be careful the company you keep. If you think you're performing some great moral good by socializing with Reynolds, then fine, but don't forget what he is. Don't be fooled by talk of black magic and evil spirits waiting for an opportunity to sink the ship. Voodoo is another crutch used by the inferior races to compensate for lack of natural intelligence and good sense."

"Aye, Captain."

Back on deck the sea seems to speak, and I strain to comprehend its complex language of wind and waves swooshing and washing against the hull. It has taken on a persona, becoming almost another member of the crew with its own moods and temperament spanning from serene contentment, to wrathful fury, to a sense of humor. As I head back to my quarters, the smell of dead fish permeates the air, and it seems now to be in an in-between phase, brewing, stirring, working its way toward something. A light rain begins to fall. Just before descending the hatch to my sleeping quarters, I turn impulsively to find Kronen staring me down from above with a sinister grin plastered on his face. I open the hatch and go down.

Before opening the door to my quarters, I stand in the cramped passage way listening to the drunk cook, Mathiassen, whose door is opposite mine, trying to make out what I can of his nightly rambling soliloquy. It is more animated than usual: "You stupid nagging whore, you think I don't know what's going on? You think I don't know he's a living, breathing demon when I see the bastard in the flesh everyday? So you'd have me take on the devil himself in the midden of the ocean, would you? Yes, yes, I'm a drunken coward, but you my dear are a stupid bitch for talking that way. The depth of your stupidity rivaled only by that of the ocean on which we sail. Let's drink to that, my dear!"

Mathiassen is now the drunk cook serving aboard the Phoenix, but between his intoxicated ramblings and a few of our conversations, I've gathered he's also a failed poet and former professor whose career ended in a burning pile of shame. His poetic flair often reveals itself during these drunken diatribes, and I've developed a habit of eavesdropping on him, hoping to catch a notable phrase or two to turn over in my head. But as I lay down to sleep on my cot, I think of his latest outburst in a different light. A living, breathing demon? It could've been Kronen or another member of the crew he was speaking of, perhaps someone from his past, completely unrelated to the ship, but I feel certain it was the captain.

Lying in the darkness of my little room, listening to the wind whine and wail, wondering where in the hell we are, I feel the need to confide in someone as the captain has confided in me.

Annoyed by the captain's admonition, it occurs to me that he's as afraid of Reynolds as Reynolds is of him. Perhaps more so. Though he may actually believe his theories about the "inferior races" I suspect what concerns him most is Reynolds' intelligence and refusal to ignore what he sees; an acknowledging of the signs. I have my own problems with Reynolds' superstitions, but I don't talk to him in order to give myself a self-congratulatory pat on the back for high morality. Rather, because he's engaging and nothing which happens on the Phoenix seems to get past him. Unlike the majority of the crew, he's sober more often than not, and despite the captain's warning I decide he's the only one aboard in whom I can safely confide.

* * *

The night before commencing our journey, we held a party aboard the ship, still docked in port. An abundance of food, whiskey and beer was consumed by captain and crew as well as several others not now among us, who—apparently hearing the festivities—invited themselves aboard for a few hours. In the spirit of the occasion, I played guitar and sang several songs on the main deck until I was too inebriated to stay in time or key. In any case, it was at this time that introductions were made and the captain gave us a summary of the voyage's purpose.

Apparently the entire enterprise was being sponsored and financed by the wealthy recluse, Halverton Woodstock, Jr. This Woodstock claimed to have evidence that a sparsely populated island in the Caribbean Sea, off the southeastern coast of Central America, held within its soil certain minerals and plant species capable of healing and restoration, unlike anything the world had seen. Woodstock, according to the captain, suffered from a rare, degenerative disease, and had become obsessed with the possibility of these remotely hidden elixirs.

Although we all indulged that first night, Mathiassen got drunker than I'd thought humanly possible. At one point he stripped down to his undergarments, climbed out to edge of the bow and threatened to jump overboard. "This life on land among men has grown rotten and foul, the sea calls me forth! The air suffocates, let me cast my lot among my faithful brothers, the dolphins and whales!"

A few of the crew and I pulled him back down onto the deck and then, at the captain's direction, dragged him down the hatch and locked him in the brig until morning. In hindsight, it was quite a fitting introduction to Mathiassen, although I've had subsequent interactions with him that were surprisingly sober and even enlightening.

It was during this episode putting Mathiassen in the brig to sober up, that I met Reynolds.

"We haven't even left port yet, and already this man has lost mind," he said, after we'd bolted the brig shut and made our way back up to the deck. A wiry black man with large intelligent eyes, there was a trace of the Caribbean in his voice.

"He seems to have lost it well before tonight. I'm Dent, by the way; Lionel Dent."

"John Reynolds," he said, extending a hand that was rough and heavy like leather, the product of years of laboring outdoors in the elements.

"Perhaps, but I still say it's a bad omen."

"Superstitious are you?"

"Oh yes, I sure am," he said, grinning. "I'm originally from Nassau. What you call 'superstitious', is to me a sign to be regarded."

"So you're saying the voyage is already doomed?"

"Not at all. Right now, just something to keep an eye on."

I suddenly sobered with the realization that once we pulled up anchor, for an untold number of months this vessel would be my entire world. There would be nowhere to escape, nowhere to run, except overboard into a cold bottomless sea.

A knot tightened in my stomach. Ashore, past the docked ships and fishing boats, lights shone in the windows of stores, buildings and hotels, and in the dwellings beyond. They looked very far away, part of some distant planet.

Reynolds seemed to sense my unease. "Hey, if I thought we were doomed, I would've already packed my bags," he said.

"Good, I'd hate to set off knowing we're done for," I said. "Guess we'll just have to keep an eye on those signs."

Kronen spent some of that night following the captain around like a jealous dog, but mostly kept to himself lurking in the corners, chewing his tobacco and spitting the juice overboard, all the while eyeing the newly assembled crew with suspicion. I was immediately made uneasy by him, something which he appeared to recognize and take pleasure in. Each time I looked at him across the deck, he'd glare back at me, grinning as if already making plans for my demise.

"Who is that strange creature, keeping to himself in the shadows," I asked Reynolds.

"That's Kronen, the first mate."

"He seems to have it in for me and I've never said a word to him."

"Kronen has it in for everybody. He's like a gray cloud that hovers about, even when there's nothing but sun and clear skies. Be glad he's keeping his distance for now."

"If he has a problem with me, I prefer to know what it is."

"Maybe you remind him of someone who licked him in a fight; maybe he doesn't like the way you walk. Some men just hate without reason."

"Christ, how long have you been attached to the ship, Reynolds?"

"This'll be my second voyage, my first with captain Melfrane."

"What happened to the last captain?"

"Captain Dryer? He fell ill. By the end of the last voyage he could barely stand. Last I heard, he was still recovering, and I don't know that they ever discovered what was ailing him. In Tahiti, we unloaded grain and iron ore and took on pearls and vanilla. When we ported, captain Dryer spent a lot of time at a brothel. I indulged as well, as did most of the crew, but Dryer disappeared for days and I believe that's where he contracted his malady. I know no more of Melfrane than you, just what we've seen and heard here tonight."

The captain appeared in good spirits that first night. After we'd assembled below in the mess room for introductions and a brief explanation of our mission, he maintained a cordial aloofness, engaging various crew members whenever he saw fit. Large and barrel-chested with a slightly bowlegged gait, he was physically imposing, the kind of man who didn't have to stop and say "excuse me," before someone got out of his way, but his formidableness transcended the mere physical. At one point he pulled me aside.

"How do you feel about your maiden voyage, Dent? Ready to take up anchor and set out to sea? I know I am. Enough of this waiting around, twiddling our thumbs, let's get on with it already!"

It was only small talk, but as we spoke I had the sense that he owned the space we occupied and

I was merely a guest visiting his personal domain. He conveyed an authority and presence that defied explanation.

"I believe you'll do well, Dent, if you can get beyond the self-doubt and indecision which weakens and freezes you. You have potential yet."

I suppose it was a backhanded complement, but unlike Kronen he seemed to have taken a liking to me and the words stirred in me a sense of obligation, a desire to stay in his good graces. My life prior to the ship was rife with failure and indirection. I yearned for an endeavor in which to prove myself, an occupation to comfortably and easily pronounce as my own. For some time I'd sensed a piece of me was missing and the captain's words engendered a belief that I'd find whatever I was looking for at sea.

"I certainly hope so, Captain," I replied, so eager for the voyage now that my heart was racing. "I'm ready to go when you are. If Mathaissen doesn't sober up, I might even have to learn to cook."

"Let's wait until we're starving before taking such dire measures," he said, slapping my back and roaring with laughter, a deep thunderous laugh that rose from his depths, causing his entire body to shake.

* * *

Milling about the deck, not touching the liquor, and repeatedly jamming his hands in his pockets, then removing them again to dangle awkwardly by his sides, was a boy who looked no more than nineteen. He wore a gray cap low over his brow and his ragged trousers and shirt hung loosely on his thin frame. His nervousness made me uncomfortable—enough so, that I approached him to see if I could help put him at ease.

"Henry," he said, once again removing his hand from his pocket to shake mine.

"Been working aboard ships for long?"

"Just a couple of years as a cabin boy, sir. Spent a year aboard the cruise liner North Star and another on the Molly Mason," he said, looking down at the deck as if he'd dropped a quarter.

"Well, you've got more experience than me."

He looked up abruptly. "This your first voyage, sir? I thought for sure I was the least experienced," he said, his mood brightening.

"I can't even tie a bowline. In fact, I was hoping once we set out, you could show me how."

"Of course. Be glad to, sir."

His uncertainty was made more prominent being in the company of men, most of whom were at least ten years older. Like me, I sensed he'd been left to his own devices from a young age and couldn't help but feel a little sorry for him. Being addressed with such deference caught me off guard, though I'd be lying if I said I disliked it.

There were two other members of the crew who immediately got my attention. They were brothers who seemed to be attached by some invisible piece of rope, as they were rarely apart. It was odd considering they were also constantly bickering and getting on one another's nerves. Not long after meeting Henry, the festivities were brought to a halt when the two of them took to shouting and cursing each other, on the verge of blows. Reynolds and I went over and got between them, trying to figure out what the hell they were so hot about.

Chapter 1

Dale and Don were big boys—strong as oxes. I was sure they were twins at first, but it turned out Dale, slightly bigger and more outgoing, was a year older. They both had large, pear shaped heads and faces that emitted perpetual expressions of confusion and distrust. I couldn't look at either for too long without wanting to laugh.

"That piece of dog shit ate my food!" Don yelled as we held them apart.

"I didn't eat his food! Why would I eat his food!" Dale yelled back.

"He ate it while I was taking a piss!"

"For godsakes," the captain said, striding over with an amused smile. "Someone get the dimwit another plate of food."

As I grabbed Dale by the upper arms, trying to move him backward, I was made aware of his brute strength. He took a step back, letting me move him away from the fracas. It was evident that he didn't really want to fight, that this was some kind of ritual he and Don occasionally engaged in to clear the air between them, or to let off steam. In a few minutes they were side by side again, talking as if nothing had happened.

During the skirmish, I'd noticed that Don was missing most of his pinky and the upper portion of the ring finger on his right hand. I'd soon learn the severed fingers were an ongoing point of tension between them: a few years before, working on a trawler, he cut off the fingers using a knife to gut fish and blamed Dale for distracting him.

Captain Melfrane cut off the whiskey and beer, then called the crew, there were maybe twenty of us in all, around him for a final speech before sending us to our quarters to get some sleep. Kronen stood straight and rigid by his side like an obedient guard dog as he spoke. "Gentleman, I hope the dire importance of this voyage has been made clear. It's crucial your duties be performed with the utmost diligence and care, as the carelessness of one puts all in danger. Disobedience will not be tolerated, the stakes are too high. If any of you have misgivings, if you believe for whatever reason that you'll be unable to perform the duties required of you, I ask that you come forward now and exit the ship, no questions asked. Tomorrow morning it will be too late."

There was silence as the lot of us craned our necks, shifted our feet and glanced sideways to see if anyone would leave. No one came forward.

"Very well."

On a lighter note, he continued, "It's of course understood that you'll be without the company of women for some time. Those with wives, girlfriends—or in some cases both—will keep them in their thoughts and hearts until we return. "The rest of you, Henry," he said, making a throat clearing noise,"will still have your hand and a jar of whale oil to keep you company."

We erupted in laughter, all except Henry who was standing next to me. I gave him a playful nudge in the ribs with my elbow, letting him know it was all in good fun, but his face reddened with shame and he jammed his hands in his trouser pockets, looking stiffly down at his boots. I believe if the captain had waited until then to ask if anyone wanted to leave, that was the last we would've seen of Henry.

The captain brought forth a big rag doll, holding it up for us to see, and continued. "This here is my lovely mistress, Sally, a faithful beacon of light to guide us on our journey. As you can plainly see, her beauty and charm is beyond compare. You're free to take her dancing or engage her in a chat, but God help you if I discover I've been cheated on."

There were a few guffaws and laughs, but they were muffled and awkward, as though no one was completely certain he was joking. There seemed an unspoken meaning to be taken from it. I couldn't stop staring at the doll. Someone had taken great care to dress her. The mop of hair made of thick yellow yarn, the dangling shapeless legs with little black shoes fitted on to the feet. She wore a modest blue dress buttoned up to the neck, and looking at her expressionless face and lifeless indifferent eyes, I got a chill.

The ceremony culminated with me leading the crew through a few songs. The captain handed me the guitar and by that time I had sobered up enough to do an adequate rendition of "Tommy's Gone Away" and then, "The Sailor Likes His Bottle-O" as my shipmates joined in. They were happily drunk and genuinely enjoying themselves.

The captain in particular was in raucous good spirits. His rich baritone distinguished itself clearly above the other voices as if he were hooked up to a megaphone, and I thought then that he could've been a professional singer. He felt the music deeply, closing his eyes and swaying slightly as he sang. Halfway through the first song, he picked up Sally, holding her close so that her lifeless head rested comfortably on his shoulder, and waltzed her around the deck with practiced ease as the crew whistled and shouted.

* * *

Before the last song ended, I found myself gazing over the heads of the crew, beyond the boundaries of the ship, at the immense expanse of water, dark and mysterious, stretching toward an ever distant horizon. I thought I saw the glimmering light of a ship moving almost imperceptibly along the horizon but the light quickly vanished leaving me to question whether I'd seen anything at all. I was full of doubt and fear, but also eager to begin the voyage. I'd spent years roaming the land, drifting from job to job, the last of which was delivering alcohol from underground distillers to discreet restaurants, back alley merchants, speakeasies and who ever else wanted to wet their pallet with a shot of whiskey, now forbidden by federal mandate. There was no shortage of demand and a suit from up the road in D.C. was starting to snoop around. I suspect he'd already caught wind of my scent, but he was far from my main concern.

The sale of liquor—and about every other illegal pursuit on the Baltimore waterfront— including gambling and prostitution, was controlled by Roland "Baby Face" Renault. As was my nature, I'd been working independently, thinking of myself as a contractor of sorts. Playing at various establishments, I'd met several whiskey and beer distillers and when one of them asked if I wanted to make some extra cash, I jumped at the opportunity with no thought I might be stepping on Renault's toes. Renault, though, made sure to place himself at the forefront of my thoughts.

One night, I'd slipped out the back of McSwain's on the waterfront after dropping off several crates of whiskey and hard cider. I was walking to the truck the distiller lent me for deliveries, when a couple of goons popped out from behind the truck for a little talk.

"Buddy, you don't deliver a single shot of whiskey in this town without giving Roland Renault his cut," the smaller one said, as the bigger one blocked my path to the door. They were almost caricatures. Both had heavy round faces and sizable guts protruding over their waste bands. They stank of cigar smoke and whiskey. "You keep it up and you'll be taking a long vacation at the bottom of Baltimore Harbor." They had me put my hands on the hood of the truck and shook me down, grabbing my wallet, spare change and a silver pocket watch I'd carried since childhood. In those moments you think of running, fighting, playing dumb, trying to talk your way out of it, but in the end a clown resorts to smartassery.

"If you wouldn't mind scratching the itch on my left knee since you're already down there fellas," I said, as they patted me down.

"Shut up, clown. You've been warned, don't let me see you 'round here again," the smaller one said. I braced myself, expecting one of them would take the opportunity to slug me before they left, but they walked off quietly which turned out to be worse.

I returned the truck and told the distiller I was quitting, but they'd gotten into my head. I'd heard too many stories about men who'd crossed Baby Face Renault: just the previous week a restaurant owner had been thrown off a fourth story balcony in downtown Baltimore. I couldn't stop imagining the kinds of depraved punishment I'd be in for if they caught me, "round here again." What did that mean, anyway? McSwain's? The waterfront? Baltimore?

Finally, I went to see Kate, as almost always I did when seeking comfort from a world that seemed to have no place for me. She was behind the counter of her family's soda shop when I waved at her through the window. She let her mother know she was taking a break, removed her apron and stepped outside.

"You must be in trouble, I swear it's the only time you come see me anymore, Lionel," she said, smoothing out her flower patterned blue dress. She was a little too tall and flatter in the chest than I preferred. A few of her front teeth were crooked and overlapping as though fighting for position in her mouth. But when she looked at me and smiled, her brown eyes growing bright and alert, my chest swelled with a rising hope, and I temporarily forgot my burdens.

"I get distracted, and lose track of time. Doesn't mean I haven't been thinking of you," I said as we walked down the avenue.

"Responsibility—it's not exactly your strong suit. You look like hell. What happened?"

Her relentless honesty was both painful and refreshing. I told her about my latest occupational crash and the run-in with Renault's goons.

"You're always doing this, taking on pursuits you know don't have any chance of succeeding. My father would hire you if you asked, you know. And I'd be able to keep an eye on you then." Her eyes softened when she said this, as though I were a wounded animal she'd found on the street and planned to nurse back to health.

"Your father hates me and thinks his little girl could do a lot better. If Renault's thugs threw me off a bridge tomorrow, he wouldn't be losing any sleep."

"You fool, stop it!" She abruptly halted and faced me. We'd turned down an unfamiliar residential street lined with redbrick tenement buildings. A group of children were in the street playing kick the can. Two old men stood on the corner contentedly smoking cigarettes. I pulled her close and planted my lips firmly on hers. She kissed me back, eagerly giving me her tongue, and my desire rose. I let my hands slide down her back, taking hold of her supple, apple shaped bottom. She detached her lips from mine, stepped back to appraise me, then gave me a hard smack across the face.

"What the hell was that about?"

"You need to make a decision, Lionel. I won't be your part-time whore, and I won't continue waiting around while you act like a child wasting your life in shady saloons with drunken degenerates."

This wasn't the comfort I'd come seeking. I tried for a moment to picture myself at work in her family's soda shop, making ice cream malts, ringing up customers. Just the idea made breathing difficult, like someone was sitting on my chest. She was a "modern woman" who wore her light brown hair short in the current fashion, and supported worker's rights, picketing in solidarity with the women garment workers in front of city hall for better pay and a shorter work week. But she also pined for a traditional marital arrangement. It was a commitment I didn't feel capable of and I decided then to make a clean break.

"Then go find someone else, Kate. Someone who wants to work in a soda shop and likes being slapped."

It wasn't the response she'd planned on and her face went blank with surprise for a second before her eyes welled up with tears. "Don't come see me anymore, Lionel," she said, softly.

I watched her turn and continue down the block with quick angry strides, walking off in the opposite

direction. I could still feel the imprint of her hand on the side of my face, but instead of
serving as confirmation of the affair's end, it was like an emblem of her love. I was walking around with her passion and belief in us tattooed on my cheek, and I found myself savoring the sensation, wishing the sting would somehow remain embedded there.

I turned back onto the avenue, trying to lose myself amongst the growing swarms of people just getting off work. Textile workers making their way home from the mills in Hampden-Woodberry, railroad men from the Northern Central Railroad Yards, steel workers, all blending together in a river that flowed steadily through the streets.

I kept telling myself it was good to know where we stood, good to have the finality that allows one to move on, but something else told me I'd made a terrible mistake. The sun had begun to set, and to stem the growing tide of regret, I hopped on a streetcar and headed for Broadway and Thames Street, where a man would have no problem finding a shady saloon full of drunken degenerates. I spent the night there, drinking myself into a state of memory obliterated numbness.

Thereafter, I avoided those venues where I played gigs and waited on table, playing instead on street corners and down at the docks for spare change. I learned to juggle and some days instead of playing guitar, I'd visit a park or stand on a corner juggling apples and oranges, or if feeling particularly brazen, knives. Other days were spent wandering around town in a directionless haze from which I couldn't seem to shake free. It was as if the early morning fog rolling in off the harbor had seeped into my body and clouded my brain. During these episodes, the most rudimentary tasks became difficult. I had trouble remembering what I'd been doing or where I'd been, just an hour before. Ordering a meal and sitting down to consume it required an inordinate amount of focus and will power. The idea of holding a conversation was unthinkable. I recall one instance during this state of mental haze when I found myself on the south side, quite far from where I was staying. As I stood on a street corner, it began to rain very hard. The street—which seconds before bustled with vendors, automobiles, horse drawn carts and pedestrians—cleared out as everyone sought cover. I alone, remained in the street as the drops pelted me, making no effort to seek refuge in one of the many shops or restaurants, or even to stand beneath the overhang of a nearby building. It wasn't that I didn't want to get out of the rain, but that I was frozen, seemingly unable to make a simple decision as to where specifically I should go. After several minutes of the drops pelting my face, soaking me through my shirt and trousers, I   embraced the wetness, wondering why anyone would run away from such refreshing bliss.

Finally, an old heavyset woman, her hair wrapped in a blue kerchief, wobbled out of a cafe holding an umbrella, trudged into the street and took me by the arm. She led me back to the cafe, sat me down at a table and brought me a hot cup of tea and a towel to dry myself. "Drink, drink," she said in a heavy accent, encouraging me like a child. I did as she said and when the rain let up, nodded at her in appreciation and made my way home.

More and more I was wandering down to the docks. I'd find a spot on the pier and watch the steamers, cargo ships, old square riggers, trawlers, tug boats. Staring out across the harbor to where the sky meets the sea, its allure and mystique would envelop me until there was a visceral feeling of being pulled forth, as though one of the tug boats had latched onto my waist and was carrying me out to sea.

It was during one of these meandering trips out to the docks that I was hired aboard The Phoenix. I'd been sitting on a bench, talking to an old-timer. When I mentioned I was looking for work, he said he'd heard the ship was looking to round out its crew for an upcoming voyage. I found it docked a mile or so from the pier, an old steamer, about 150 feet stern to bow, I guessed. You could tell she was an older ship, probably renovated a time or two to keep it afloat. The wooden planks of her hull had been reinforced with iron, and barnacles and mollusk grew prosperously at the waterline. The porting bridge was down and I stepped aboard, uninvited.

"Who the hell are you?" a voice called out when I was on deck.

It turned out to be the captain's voice. When I told him why I'd come, he sat me down right there on the deck for an impromptu interview; except it wasn't really an interview, but more an excuse for him to spout an opinion on everything from prohibition to the segregating of the races to a disgust with what he called the "cowardice of modern man." He asked if I had experience aboard a ship, quickly read my anxious silence, and answered his own question. "It doesn't matter, really. There're mates who've spent most of their lives at sea I wouldn't allow to set foot on this ship. It comes down to character, dedication, loyalty." He took a moment to look me over and his gaze settled on my hands.

"You've got the hands of a midtown banker," he said with scorn, and I looked down, self-consciously examining them—had he not noticed my calloused fingers?

His tone lightened a bit. "That's alright, we'll make a man of you yet, Dent."

There was something paternal about him. I sensed he wanted to mold me into something better and more capable. What new kind of man might be shaped and honed under his guidance? For a moment, I saw myself straddling the bow of a great ship during a nor'easter, directing the crew, calling out coordinates to the helmsman.

"What's the pay?"

"You'll be fairly compensated."

He could've offered to pay me in fish heads and sea salt. I needed something to aspire to, something to redirect my attention away from Kate and potential run-ins with Renault's goons—an entire new world to render the present one obsolete. That he might have an ulterior motive for bringing me aboard didn't occur to me, nor do I believe it would've mattered, at least not then. There was nothing keeping me tied to the land anymore, and like Mathiassen, I was ready to cast my lot upon the sea and prove my worth aboard the Phoenix.

Chapter 2

The following morning, I'm on the deck, working through my routine. The sky is clear blue and sunlight glistens on the ocean surface with a playful calm. There are days when the sea appears completely devoid of life, as if all its creatures have conspired to avoid the ship. Not a single bird or fish to be seen. But on this morning, a school of porpoise swims by, their sleek dark forms effortlessly breaking the ocean's surface before submerging again. Pelicans, traveling in a group of five, fly over, continuing onward in search of their next meal. I would like to see some whales but have seen only one so far, and then it wasn't really a whale I'd seen, but the spray from its spout shooting skyward like a geyser.

The ease and grace with which these creatures navigate the sea serves as a reminder that we're merely visitors here. At times, the sea froths with anger, pounding the deck with windrain, its great swells tossing the ship about like a toy as though offended anyone could be foolish enough to test their mettle upon it, and I think with horror how the rusted iron hull and slowly rotting keel boards, are all that stand between us and a bottomless gorge teeming with beasts capable of crushing a man with the flip of a tail.

As I'm cleaning the deck, Dale comes up the steps from below. He walks directly to the ships edge, casually takes hold of the guard rail, and retches overboard.

"Morning, Dent," he says, smiling at me when he's done. He and Don consume profound amounts of alcohol and seeing one of them in the morning depositing the contents of their stomach into the ocean, is as common as witnessing other crew members drink their coffee.

Later, taking a break from my duties, I see Reynolds stern side taking his break; and join him. We lean against the hull, looking over the rail, out at the expanse of ocean behind us. I'm not sure how to broach the subject of the captain when Reynolds says: "Sometimes I wonder if the captain's growing unhinged."

"Yeah? What have you observed?"

"Well, first off, we see less and less of him. And when he does decide to grace us with his presence, it's usually to lash out at the crew, making unfounded accusations."

We talk in whispers, periodically turning our heads in case the captain should appear without warning like a specter.

"Yesterday, he lit into Mathiassen, accusing him of trying to poison his food. He threatened to throw the drunk fool in the brig and keep him locked up till we return home."

"Poison his food? We've never even seen the man eat anything," I say, growing annoyed.

"Shhh, lower your voice," Reynolds says, peering over his shoulder. "We haven't seen him eat, but if he's a man like you say, then he must. Probably has Mathiassen bring him his meals privately."

"But why?"

"Hell if I know. The captain's a strange bird and getting stranger."

"Last night I heard Mathiassen through his door. He was upset, going on about "that demon" and bickering with his imaginary woman about not having the courage to do anything. That might explain it. Did he say anything to Melfrane?"

"They were arguing, growing more and more heated until the captain said something that made Mathiassen go quiet real quick. He broke off into some drunk muttering I couldn't make out, then fell silent."

I'm about to tell Reynolds the captain has enlisted me as his informant when something stops me. Somehow, either by reading a change in my gestures and voice, or by that inexplicable second sight that allows him to hear and know things he shouldn't, he'll know. And once he knows, I fear his wrath will be directed at me; a wrath whose power I prefer not to imagine. But this isn't the only thing keeping my mouth shut. I genuinely don't want to betray his confidence and tell myself there might be reasons for his recent erratic behavior, perhaps very good ones.

"He's always made veiled threats, that's been his style since the day we set sail. And Mathiassen isn't exactly trustworthy. Who knows what depraved thing he might've done to set the captain off."

Reynolds shoots me a sideways glance, then gazes back out at sea. "The threats aren't so veiled anymore, they're direct and becoming more serious. And what about his disappearing act?"

"He looked pale and kind of off the last time I saw him. Maybe he's sick with something and doesn't want to spread it to the crew, or thinks if we see him in his weakened state he'll lose control of the ship," I say, half believing my own words.

"I don't like it, Dent. Something isn't right."

"You're foolish, jumping to conclusions based on superstition and black magic. We can't turn the ship around every time the wind whips someone's hat overboard, or one of the crew shaves his beard. No one's been harmed, we're all still here, and I expect we'll be reaching the island any day now."

Reynolds shoots me another glance, this one brimming with disdain and not a little bit of disappointment. When I look over my shoulder again, there's Kronen, walking toward us with a sinister grin. We quickly agree to continue the conversation at a later time.

Kronen spits a brown load of tobacco juice over the rail before stopping directly in front of us. "What are you ladies gossiping about," he says, his grin widening across a broad face, beneath a pig like snout of a nose.

"Oh, you know, Kronen, we were just discussing what an honor it would be if you came over and joined us."

He sheds the grin and turns toward me. "Watch yourself, Dent. You weren't nothin' on land and you're less at sea. You're a fraud; a singing dancing fraud. I see it, the captain sees it, the whole crew sees it. I'd put your chances of making it back to port in one piece as next to none." He spits out another brown wad and walks off.

Reynolds moves off as well, tending to his work. I remain, looking out at the bright rippling ocean, trembling slightly, trying to get hold of my emotions. Kronen has touched an exposed nerve and I'd felt a strong impulse to shove him over the guardrail. Understanding I'm capable of such murderous urges has shaken me, leaving me to wonder if captain Melfrane isn't the only one who might be growing unhinged.

After only a month at sea, it required no great imagination to understand how a man could lose his bearings, could come unmoored, so to speak; or if he was already teetering on the brink, how he might be carried over the edge, kicking and screaming. The previous year, there'd been a newspaper story about a merchant marine aboard a cargo ship bound for the Adriatic Sea. One night, he took a machete from the galley and lopped off both ears of a sleeping shipmate. A few of his fellow sailors subdued him before he could do more damage. It wasn't his first voyage and he hadn't done anything beforehand to indicate he was on the verge of snapping. As they carried him down to the brig, they asked why he'd done it. He told them that the man whose sleeping cot had been a foot away from his own, was too nosy and needed to be taught to mind his own business.

Merchant mariners weren't the most stable lot to begin with, and it was well known many crimps hired the least experienced and most desperate among them because they could pay them less. I'd begun to suspect that the captain had hired me not in spite of my lack of experience, but because of it. The crew was mostly an assembly of drifters, misfits and drunks one had to strain to picture living well adjusted lives ashore. If on an empty city street, you happened to see one of them walking toward you, you'd strongly consider crossing to the other side.

In essence, we were here because we hadn't any other options. Mix in the cramped living quarters, awful body odor (I'm certain I could identify a few of my shipmates blindfolded) and the desolation sometimes evoked by an endless, flat expanse of ocean, and you wondered why more men didn't unravel.

After a minute, a lone seagull flies over, crossing the bow of the ship port to starboard. I've seen him before, always traveling solo, and identify him by a dark streak on his left wing which looks to me like a birthmark. At the moment he passes above, he lets out a friendly cry and in spite of my jabbing Reynolds for his superstitious absurdities, I take the gull's appearance as a good omen and my nerves begin to calm.

Not a small portion of my duties aboard the Phoenix involve assisting Mathiassen below deck in the galley as he prepares the meals. I'm not much of a cook and do what he asks of me, but my main responsibility is to keep an eye on him, making sure he doesn't set the ship on fire, either by accident or with intent. "Sprinkle these with some garlic salt, grease four large pans and stick em in the oven, Dent. 350 degrees," he says, later that afternoon, pointing to the stuffed hens he's prepared for dinner. He then uncorks a bottle of cheap red wine he's already halfway through, and takes a long pull. "If I pass out, take 'em out again in three hours."

I do as he says, eyeing a large butcher's cleaver which hangs on the wall next to the ovens. Its over sized, freshly sharpened blade, always makes me a bit nervous.

Mathiassen's actually a decent cook and I surmise that the captain with his upper crust tastes hired him aboard in part for this reason, but I'm beginning to sense there's a history between the two.   "Tell me how you came to know the captain, Mathiassen, how you came to be on the ship," I say.

"What the hell for?" he says, scowling. "That's a mighty presumptuous question, Dent. Down right invasive, if I don't say so. I liked you better when you were aloof and polite."

"I thought a little conversation might help pass the time."

"So might singing, or getting drunk and passing out. Time's an odd animal, Dent. We all have our own clocks, each ticking at its own pace. Mine's been broken for a while now. Couldn't tell you what day or even month it is, and honestly I no longer give a damn."

"Why's that?"

"Why's what?"

"You no longer give a damn."

"Christ, you think everything has to have a reason," he says, putting the wine bottle down on the metallic counter top. He has a wild mop of graying curly hair and a lean face with a strong jaw sprouting a handful of whiskers from the chin.

"It doesn't?"

"What's the reason the lot of us, you, me and the rest of the crew, are stuck on a ship in the middle of the ocean, captained by a madman," he says, for the first time turning his gaze directly upon me. His eyes are lively now, searching.

"Reynolds said he heard you and the captain arguing about something yesterday, said the captain sounded pretty hot."

"A man can't have a thought on this ship without someone else hearing it. You can tell Reynolds to mind his own damn business," he says, turning away and reaching for the bottle. "Yes, we know each other, unfortunately," he says quietly, before raising the bottle to his lips and taking a long swig. I want to ask him why the captain thinks his food may be poisoned, but he walks away and sits down in the far corner of the galley, letting me know that for now, the conversation is over.

* * *

That evening after dinner a group of us remain on the mess deck to socialize for a bit.

"I heard the women outnumber the men ten to one," Dale says.

"Yeah, and they walk around in the nude, nothing but little seashells covering their nipples. At night, they skinny dip in the lagoons, wishing there was a real man around that could satisfy em," Don adds.

"A real man?" says an older shipmate who works in the engine room. Like the other firemen, his face and arms appear permanently charred by the tons of coal they fed into the boilers each day. "Well, that would count out you two dolts."

"Stuff it old timer," Dale says. "You're just sore cause your little gentleman don't work no more."

"A real man," he continues. "That's probably what you tell each other at night while your pullin' on each other's pud."

More and more, the talk was turning to the island of our destination and because so little was known of it, the crew had taken to filling in the blanks with self-styled fairy tales: it was inhabited by beautiful, sex-starved women, serene mountain lakes full of fish that jumped right into your boat, and waterfalls. Who could blame them? It helped keep a man sane with something beyond an endless sea to hope for. I had my own closely guarded hopes and the island had even seeped into my dreams on occasion. But I could see it setting up for grave disappointment and took it upon myself to temper expectations.

"For all we know, the place is full of hostile natives and poisonous snakes," I say.

"Christ Dent, don't be such a downer," Dale says.

"You guys talk like we're heading for the Garden of Eden. You might want to ease up on the fantasies."

After washing the dishes, I make my way up the companionway to help the deckhands ridding the main deck of wash, clearing out the accumulation of crud, muck and dirt left by men and sea alike. Others are tasked with tying down the foremast and folding ropes. Henry is there. It's his turn on watch duty and as he stands atop the forecastle, looking pale and dazed, I wonder if perhaps he's ill. Though he's suffered admirably without complaint, the voyage has not been kind to him. Already thin, he's undergone a noticeable loss of weight as he seems to have trouble holding down any food, and when recently I found him standing on deck with his eyes closed, he admitted he'd been unable to sleep at night. His youth and innocence make him an easy target for the jibes and teasing of the crew, and his tendency to take it personally only makes it worse. If that wasn't enough, the captain has taken an apparent dislike to him, on a few occasions going out of his way to reprimand him in front of the other men. I suspect the captain views him as weak and cowardly, traits he not only finds offensive, but which arouse in him an unchecked cruelty.

In addition to the loss of weight, there's been a change in Henry's demeanor. Perhaps as a way of combating the jibes and reprimands, he's grown more aloof, at times drifting off into his own little world until he's unaware of what's going on around him and one has to call his name several times to grab his attention. It comes off almost as rebellion, although, I believe, an unconscious one.

We work this way for maybe half of an hour. It is a pleasant evening. The seas are tame and the setting sun reflects off the small ocean crests with a serene warmth. I squat with a bucket, collecting deck wash and dumping it over the side of the ship. I've come to take satisfaction in the daily tasks required to keep the ship properly afloat. There's something about the physical nature of the work under the elements, and understanding our survival depends upon it, which quiets the mind and lifts the spirit. It ties the lot of us together until we seem greater than the sum of our parts.

Lowering myself again with the bucket, I look up to find the captain standing astride the bridge deck, just below the pilot house. Hands on hips, head tilted slightly up and forward, he stands unmoving, statuesque. His slacks are tucked neatly into polished black leather boots that conclude an inch below the knee. For a moment, it's as though he's become an inanimate part of the ship, like the keel or anchor. But he soon moves slightly forward, dispelling the illusion. Something has demanded his attention and he cranes his neck forward, peering out intently, raising a hand and holding it against his brow to narrow his gaze.

Curious to know what has his interest, I rise from my squatting position and follow his gaze until my own falls on Henry. He's still atop the forecastle, standing in the little watch nest, but he's now holding a spool of string wrapped around what looks like a piece of driftwood. The string reaches high above the ship, and attached to the end is a kite made of white and green rags, flapping in the light wind. "Henry, you fool," I say under my breath. Wanting to give warning of the gale about to engulf him, I search the deck for an object to throw at him, but it's too late. The captain is walking in his direction, ignoring the rest of the crew who—now aware of his presence—suspend their duties to watch.

About ten yards away, the captain halts and stares up at the little watch deck. Oblivious, Henry continues flying his homemade rag kite, his back still to the captain and to the rest of us waiting to see how this will resolve. For the first time, I fully comprehend that he's little more than a child, inventing distractions as a child will to soften the hard realities of life.

The first week after pulling up anchor, a few of us were talking on the main deck when Henry expressed an interest in the ship's mechanical workings, wondering aloud if the engine was able to continue churning and pumping on its own without anyone there to mange it. The chief engineer, a man named Crispen, was there and he grew suddenly very grave. "The little ones are always down in the engine room, working day and night."

"The little ones?" Henry said.

"Yes of course, the elves," Crispen said.

"Elves?"

"Of course. You don't really think the engine is left unattended, do you? The engine team has to sleep and without the help of our elf friends, we'd be doomed."

"Yeah elves," Henry said laughing, but the rest of us were now playing along, somberly nodding in agreement.

"It's not commonly known, but it's true," another man, said.

"But there's no such thing," Henry said uneasily.

"Go and see for yourself," Crispen said, encouraging him to descend into the engine room and look. "Go on."

He hesitated a moment, and then to our surprise, walked over and opened the hatch to the engine room. "They're very shy and like to hide in the way back, in the wheel wells behind the pistons. Try not to scare them," Crispen called out, before he went down.

He spent nearly half an hour searching around in the engine room before popping up through the hatch again.

"So, did you introduce yourself?" Crispen said, as we laughed.

Henry's face reddened, but soon he too was laughing and I thought then there was some hope for him after all. It was a dry, forced laugh, but at least he'd made the attempt at self-deprecation. It was much more likely to endear him to the crew than his tendency to brood, which only put a target on his back. From then on the men took to calling him "Elf". You could tell by his smirk that he wasn't crazy about the name, but he responded to it and his over-sized ears made it all the more fitting.

I'm thinking of the elf incident when the captain pulls a revolver from his waistband, takes careful aim of Henry's kite and blows the rags out of the air with one shot. The report of the revolver suspends in the air as rag fragments drop out of the clear evening sky. Henry turns now, looking at the captain below.

"Get the hell down here you little dimwit," he says, and Henry descends with timid, slow steps as though debating whether it might be more prudent to remain where he is. Finally on the deck, he stands facing the captain.

Silently glaring, the captain backhands him across the side of the face. A few of the men let out audible moans and there's grumbling. Henry slowly brings his head back to face the captain, then touches his bottom lip to find a trickle of blood.

"You pathetic excuse for a human being, what in god's name are you doing? The ship's safety is placed under your watch and you make a mockery of it with your careless stupidity. Are you too dull to realize how irresponsible you've been? I shot your kite, but understand, I thought good and hard about shooting you instead. At least the rags could've served some use, I ought to remedy the mistake of having ever allowed you aboard."

At this, he again unholsters the revolver and holds it at his side. Henry appears about to faint. His eyes close for a few seconds, then open, as though going in and out of consciousness. I notice the large stain on the front of his trousers, then the trickle of urine exiting out the bottom of his pants leg. I want to step forward and say something—the captain has gone too far— but like the rest of the crew, I'm frozen; open-mouthed in shock.

The captain returns the firearm to his waistband holster.

"Captain, I'll take him down to the brig," Kronen says. Making a show of his loyalty, he'd walked up behind the captain during the exchange, and now as he speaks, there's a hint of joy in his voice that quickly tightens my jaw.

The captain raises a hand, not turning to face Kronen. "No, he'll continue on watch now for twenty-four hours, this time. Perhaps it'll teach him to treat his duties with serious regard."

Henry, understanding his punishment, has gotten a hold of himself enough to begin making his way back up the steps to the watch nest. The captain turns and retraces his steps along the deck, passing the rest of us, still frozen where we stand, afraid to move. Suddenly he stops and faces us. "Let this serve as a warning to the rest of you. Insubordination will not be tolerated aboard this ship and the next one to challenge the sanctity of this commandment will be locked in the brig for the remainder of the voyage."

He looks about the faces of the crew for a moment, determines the message has been fully absorbed and continues on. As he passes me, he slows,

catching my glance for a second with a look I spend the
rest of the evening trying to interpret.

* * *

That night, I lie on my cot listening to the ship
creak and groan. I don't want to interfere; Henry after
all, has brought this on himself and I never signed up
to be his guardian. Yet, this forfeiting of obligation
causes a gnawing shame to twist in my gut like a dull
blade, and I start to think my inaction will devour me
until nothing is left. If I'd intervened, I tell myself, the
captain would've turned the gun on me, but I don't
believe it. I can't shake the sense that the look he gave
me was a challenge, a dare to step forward and act, as
if he knew he was wrong, perhaps intentionally so, in
order to know if my loyalty to him would trump the
desire to "perform some moral good."

Regardless of whether I've passed the captain's
test, I've failed my own, once again shackled into
submission by an indecision which plagues me like a
disease.

Needing to redeem myself, and keep the
situation from spiraling into chaos, I make my way
through the tunnel of berthing compartments beneath
the main deck, where the men are stowed away for the
night. The berthing compartments are adjoined to the
forecastle doors which remain open, letting the ocean
air circulate below to cool the overheated compartments
and lower deck. The issue is that this also allows the
seas into the ships interior so that everything is wet and
water accumulates, giving life to mold, rot and germs
until half the crew is coughing and sneezing. Whether
to keep the doors open or shut is an ongoing argument
among the crew and as I splash through the still water,

hearing the coughs of men through the compartment doors, I find myself siding with the doors shut faction.

As I reach the end of the passage , the last door opens and Reynolds pops his head out.

"Dent—"

"How'd you know it was me?"

"Because you're as quiet as a whale in a pond." He gestures for me to follow him into his compartment and I do so, closing the door behind me.

The little room, lit by an oil lamp, is well kept, but then there isn't much to keep: a bureau, small desk and chair, and his cot. He sits on the cot and I take the desk chair. Several books, covering subjects such as philosophy, mathematics and world history, sit on the desk and I wonder how he's able to reconcile his intellectual pursuits with his superstitions. Perhaps he feels no need to.

"Well," he says, "if you still had any doubts about the captain being unhinged, that display with Henry this evening should have put an end to them. He's a direct threat to the safety of the crew."

"I'm going to see him now. He crossed a line and it needs to be addressed."

"Yeah? What do you plan to say to him?"

"I don't know exactly, but he needs to know what he did to Henry was wrong. The men are grumbling louder, growing more unsettled. If he keeps tightening his grip, there'll be a full on rebellion."

"What's to stop him from making an example out of you like he did Henry?"

"He trusts me. He's enlisted me to find out if any of the crew are conspiring against him."

"What? You're working for him then?"

"No, not really. I mean, he is the captain, we're all working for him. What was I going to tell him?"

Reynolds face tenses and he sits up straighter on the cot. "Working under maybe, but not for. Who or what a man works for—his true loyalty—is a whole nother matter. I'm starting to wonder where your loyalty lies, Dent."

"I was going to tell you this morning before Kronen decided to show up. Come on, if I were the captain's agent, would I be sitting here talking to you about it?"

Reynolds thinks about that for a few seconds, then sighs. "I suppose not."

"I believe the captain can still be reasoned with, made to understand if he continues down this road, he'll lose the ship. He's nothing if not smart."

"What was reasonable about what we saw? You sound eager to lick his boots like he stepped in a custard pie, not reason with him. He understands perfectly what he's doing; that's the problem. We should've reached this so-called island a week ago."

"How do you know that? I'm not sure what month it is, never mind how long we've been at sea."

"Thirty three days," he says, reaching forward to open the top drawer of the desk. He pulls out a small notepad and shows me a page where he's marked off each day since we left Baltimore with an X. Trained as a carpenter, he's the ship handyman and between us on the wall hangs a level, hand saw, and chisel. The ship is an unending restoration project: leaks sprouting in the hull needing to be patched, eroded planks to be dislodged and replaced, chairs and tables to rebuild. Atop the desk is a photograph of Reynolds with his wife, son and daughter dressed in their Sunday best, staring solemnly back at the camera. If he came upon something interesting, an exotic bird feather or piece of driftwood he could scoop out of the ocean, he saved it as a souvenir for his kids. He rarely spoke of his family, but it was obvious who it was that he was working for. Seeing the picture, I grow envious, imagining how it is to

have people eagerly awaiting your return; people who miss you. I think longingly of Kate, with the idea that if we ever reach this island, I'll find an exotic souvenir to bring back to her with the hope our relationship might be repaired.

"You think he made it up?"

"I don't know. Even if it exists, he's not seeking it for the reasons he gave us."

"When I spoke with him yesterday, he mentioned you."

Reynolds raises his eyebrows and his big eyes grow bigger.

"He mentioned your superstitions, seemed to believe you're familiar with the black magic. How would he even know that?"

"The only way is if he's familiar with it himself."

I stand and start for the door.

"Hold on," Reynolds says, rising from the cot. He moves to the desk, pulls open the bottom drawer and takes out a little cloth bag. "Take this," he says, holding it out in his big leathery hand.

"What is it?"

"For protection and good luck."

I take the bag and peer inside at a few nondescript looking rocks. "Great, thanks Reynolds," I say, putting the bag in my pocket. "Should we do a chant to conjure up the spirits?"

He sneers and gives an unpleasant grin. I walk out, ascend the stairs to the deck and make my way down another hatch to the galley.

The kitchen is dark and I move carefully, trying not to send any pans or skillets crashing to the floor. Earlier, we'd had chicken soup and biscuits; it wasn't Mathiassen's finest performance and I was sure there'd be plenty left over.

"Arrhh!" a voice calls out as my foot thuds against a limp object, sending me flailing down to the hard floor. Sitting up, I see Mathiassen lying in the middle of the floor, jarred out of his drunken slumber.

"What the hell are you doing, Mathiassen? Go to your damn room if you need to pass out."

"Ah, it was such a lovely dream. You're a dream killer, Dent; a certified thief. What else do I have anymore but these dreams?"

"Why are you still here?" I say, picking myself up.

"I'm in no condition to wrestle with your philosophical propositions, Dent. Oh my dear looked most beautiful tonight. Elegant and beautiful in her evening gown she was, before you chased her away. Find me a bottle that'll bring her back. Go on, put yourself to use."

Trying to talk to him in this state is pointless. I find the cauldron of soup, now cold, scoop some out with the ladle and fill a bowl. From a tray on the counter, I grab a biscuit, smear on some butter, wrap it in a napkin and put it in my pocket. Holding the bowl, I walk past Mathiassen and ascend the steps. Just as I reach the hatch, he says something unintelligible and erupts in a mad roar of laughter.

Walking the deck, the sea is eerily calm. The ship's engine is shut down so Crispen and the firemen can rest for the night. The old foremast sail, rarely used, has been raised, but there's not a ripple and the ship is rendered nearly motionless. I pass the bridge deck and pilot house situated at ship's midpoint and ahead, I see Henry on the watch deck, illuminated by the same light which lit Kronen the night before. I climb the ladder taking care not to spill the soup, and join him on the deck, barely able to fit the two of us. He emerges from his dazed exhaustion long enough to give me a quizzical look, uncertain whether I'm there to throw him overboard, or to help.

"The lip is a little swollen but it doesn't look too bad," I say, and immediately, he touches his mouth with his fingers as though needing to confirm what I've told him.

I hold up the bowl of soup, then pull the biscuit out of my pocket, shedding the napkin with a flick of the wrist like a bad magic trick. "Look, something to eat. Not Mathiassen's best work, but it'll have to do."

He looks at me again with uncertainty, then grabs the bowl, holds it to his mouth and drains it, hands the bowl back to me, takes the biscuit and scarfs that down.

"What were you thinking, flying a kite on watch duty? You had to know it would anger him."

"I didn't think he was watching. I didn't see the captain for a few days. I made it from string I found on deck and parts of handkerchiefs I cut in pieces and tied together. It was a good kite, but the captain didn't like it very much."

"No, it appears the captain's not much a fan of kites."

"The captain doesn't like me much. Do you know why the captain hates me, Dent?" The question takes me aback. He looks at me imploringly, as though I'm guarding a secret that will remedy the situation.

"I don't think he really hates you, Henry," I say, fishing for an answer. "As men grow older, they develop certain quirks, triggers that set them off for no apparent reason, at the drop of a hat. It can be a particular word or noise, like a bottle breaking, or something they've seen, like a kite, that reminds them of something they'd rather not be reminded of."

"Why would a kite set the captain off?"

I feel myself about to get sucked down a rabbit hole of half truths and lies I won't soon be able to climb out of, and wonder how long Henry can last out here before growing so tired and weak that he tumbles into the sea. Not that long, I decide.

"I don't know, but you've been up here long enough. It's time to head down and get some rest." As soon as the words are out of my mouth, something tightens in my chest. Henry seems to grasp it as well.

"Huh? But what about the captain? What will he do when he finds out?"

"He's not here now, Henry. He won't know."

"But the captain sees everything, he's always watching, even when you think he isn't." My belief in these words sends a chill through me, but I persist. "If he does find out, you can tell him I told you to come down."

He looks skeptical, and I think he'd rather remain here stranded in the watch nest than meet the captain's wrath again. But when I turn and lower myself down the steps, he follows.

On the deck, we're about to head back to the berthing compartments when Kronen steps out from behind the pilot house bridge. I hadn't noticed him when I'd passed it.

"What in the hell you think you're doing, Dent?"

"None of your business, Kronen," I say, no longer bothering to mask my disgust with him.

"The hell it isn't. God damned insubordination is what it is. You take him right back up there, or I'll be letting Captain Melfrane know what you're up to."

"That's alright, I'm about to let him know myself," I say, brushing past him, close enough to get a good whiff of his tobacco-marred breath.

"You might as well take yourself down to the brig and lock yourself in, Dent! Cause that's where you gonna end up!" he yells after us.

I walk Henry to the aft side sleeping compartment hatch, open it and watch him go down. When I return my attention to the deck, Kronen is gone.

I continue towards the bow and Captain Melfrane's cabin. Before running into Kronen, I hadn't given any thought about whether to tell the captain I'd put an end to Henry's watch. I hadn't known I would do it until it was done. Something tells me he already knows—or at least suspects it—but this is beside the point. He will want me to acknowledge the fact to prove I'm not conniving behind his back. When I reach the hatch, I stand hovering above it, my head swimming with the growing list of issues I wish to discuss—why we haven't yet reached the island, the growing frustration and brooding of the crew, the incident with Henry.

After a brief slumber, the revitalized winds are picking up force and the ship dips and rocks over the sea's growing crests. I remain there hovering, my boots welded to the deck by indecision; it isn't too late to turn around, head back to my quarters and for a few hours, wrap myself in a blanket of sleep.

Finally, I extract my feet from the deck and descend so that I now stand outside the captain's oval door. Less than twenty-four hours earlier I stood in the exact same spot, and yet it feels like months have passed. Light is visible through the door crack along the floor. I raise my hand, knock three times and wait.

Chapter 3

After letting me in, the captain settles into his makeshift throne and I again sit uncomfortably in the wicker chair, facing him. He smiles at me knowingly, as though expecting my arrival.

"Well, well, Dent, it seems our meetings are becoming routine."

"I'm sorry to bother you, Captain," I begin, annoyed by the meekness of my words, "but there are a few things that need to be addressed before they grow out of control."

"Dent, you don't cease to surprise me," he says, sounding amused. "Just when I think you're little more than a weak minded stooge, you show some gravitas. I assume you've come to talk about what happened with Henry. You don't agree with my disciplinary measures, or perhaps with my leadership in general."

"Well, I—"

"Putting aside for a second the fact what you think of them doesn't really matter, allow me to explain something. The world is made of two basic types: those who relentlessly obtain and wield power and those who yield to it; who not having the wherewithal to direct themselves, desire consciously or unconsciously to be directed and ordered about. Furthermore, you're born one or the other with no in between. As you've by now figured out, I belong to the former group while Henry and the rest of the crew fall comfortably in the latter."

"But why be so rigid, punishing them for innocent mistakes? The crew have little room to breathe and grow more frustrated by the day. Henry is struggling; he barely eats or sleeps and hardly knows what he's doing half the time."

"Because if I don't step forward to exercise the control and discipline that's been entrusted me as captain of this ship, someone else will. I prefer it be me. As to Henry, I disagree. He knew well what he was doing, was by his blatant disobedience, begging to be disciplined, and so I obliged him. Perhaps he didn't expect the type or severity of it, but one rarely does."

"I told him he could come down from the watch nest," I mention casually, as though noting a change in the weather.

"And by that, you're expecting to achieve what?"

"He looked sickly and weak; I was afraid he might fall overboard."

"He was sick and weak long before my reprimand, before ever setting foot on this ship. Suffering on watch duty was an opportunity for him to build some strength of character. One way or another, the weak and dumb will be weeded out. I'm only speeding up the process, helping it along, if you will."

It's clear I won't change his opinion on Henry. It seems for the captain everything besides the accumulation of power is tossed aside like dirty deck wash.

"We've been at sea over a month, when will we see this so called island," I say.

"Very shortly, I think. You ought to try taking a leap of faith now and then, Dent; it does the spirit good, and perhaps then you'd be able to make a decision. I suppose relieving Henry of his watch duty was a start, even if I don't fully agree with the reasoning or resulting action."

Ah ha—so I'm not crazy to think he was issuing a challenge. But this begs an unsettling question: is he attempting to take me under his wing, grooming me as a kind of apprentice? I struggle with the idea only briefly before strange things start to happen.

I normally made a point of meeting the captain's gaze for no more than a few seconds before looking away. On this occasion though, I steady my eyes on his, and the cabin seems to fall away. His voice drops until I'm hardly aware of the meaning of the words, focused almost wholly on their sound, as though they're being filtered through a musical instrument. His eyes are unblinking and the irises, half hidden by the lids, slowly begin to rotate.

I grow sleepy, struggling to keep my own eyes open.

Weaving in and out of consciousness I become intensely aware of an itch on my scalp, but when I attempt to scratch it, my arm won't move! I try with the left arm and that one is also rendered useless, hanging limp at my side. The captain sits on his throne, no longer speaking, staring straight ahead into some unknowable void. In a panic I try to rise but I'm melded to the chair. I remember the bag of stones from Reynolds in my pocket, but there's no way to get to them, and even if I could, what was I supposed to do with them?

I begin hyperventilating. The ability to speak aloud has left me and I fear I'll soon pass out. After some minutes my breathing calms and I focus my attention on various items within the room: Sally, sitting atop the bureau; the tribal wood carvings and artifacts on the captain's desk; his bed and nightstand on the far side of the cabin, a circular window which looks out at the sea now shrouded in darkness. A healthy-sized spider crawls up the wall behind the captain and wedges itself in a ceiling crevice. It must've come aboard while we were still in port, no more aware than the rest of us what it was getting into.

It isn't until the captain speaks again, that I turn my attention back to him.

"Allow me to tell you about myself, and you'll better understand the origins of my beliefs," he begins, telling of his upbringing, the harsh trials of his youth and how through resolve and ingenuity, he was able to overcome them. I hear his voice clearly, perfectly. Except he's no longer speaking aloud! His eyes are still half closed, staring past me in a catatonic like state, while I search his face for some movement, the slightest opening and closing of his mouth to explain what I'm hearing, but the lips are firmly sealed.

The sound of his voice in my head is casual and ordinary, the same volume and tone that travels aloud through the air. He talks of how he never knew his real father and his mother— in a rush to marry and obtain stability—took up with a farmer who drank and beat him with a leather belt. At first he cried and blubbered helplessly during these whippings, but at some point he learned through the focusing of his mind, that he could control his reactions and the amount of pain he felt.

"I advanced to where I could both experience pain and separate myself from it, hovering above myself at a comfortable distance watching as an objective observer. So much of it, you see, is expectation. Most people, when they've been hit, immediately go down because they think it's what they're supposed to do. 'I must be injured and therefore unable to respond,' they tell themselves. God forbid a little blood is shed—they're libel to work themselves into hysteria and pass out. Take as an example our friend Henry yesterday, though surprisingly he never went to the ground. Someone accustomed to being hit knows otherwise.

"After a time, I started assessing the blows being delivered upon me as a critic reviews a show or meals at a restaurant: 'that one was rather weak, lacking the preparation to achieve the full effect; that one was sloppy and unfocused, causing the belt to miss me almost completely.' Mind you, I was only ten years old. Eventually, I was able to close the divide between pain and pleasure and experience the thrashing of the leather against my skin as an invigorating confirmation that I was truly alive."

His step-father, not understanding why he was no longer crying out or expressing any pain, would continue striking him until frustrated and exhausted from swinging the belt, would drop it and stagger out of the barn to load up on more liquor. When a punishment no longer elicited the desired response, he would try something new: locking him in a shed for days with only water; working him from dawn to dusk with barely a break, which he would then teach himself to endure.

"Of course it wasn't my step-father's intent—he was far too dull to foresee such things—but the punishments only made me stronger and stronger."

This self-control and discipline allowed him to overcome almost any obstacle and why, I suppose, he had so little tolerance for weakness or "the cowardice of modern man." His step-father eventually drank himself to death and, so he claimed, at the age of twelve, he took over the farm and successfully ran it for several years. He'd always had a yearning for the sea and eventually made his way to the coast in search of work aboard a ship.

I had no idea what to make of any of this. It seemed unlikely at best, and very possibly a complete crock; something concocted to build up the aura of mystery surrounding him, as if there weren't enough of that already. It left me annoyed. Perhaps if someone else had told it, I'd have been more sympathetic, but I'd grown impatient with the facades, the intentional vagueness, the misdirection. Fatherly captain, elusive mystic, greedy sadist—who the hell was he? Complex layered upon complex, persona masking persona, I questioned whether Melfrane was in fact his real name. And yet, with the power of a savant or ancient shaman, he'd rendered my body immobile, and was communicating telepathically. I couldn't completely dismiss any of what he'd told me.

As a way of lowering his guard, my first instinct, even in this incapacitated state, was to amuse, but I no longer had it in me. When the voyage first began, after dinner or during leisure time, I'd play songs and juggle for the crew on the mess deck. But those occasions had grown fewer and fewer. "Play us a song, Dent!" shipmates would call out, and I'd invent some excuse not to oblige—I had to finish cleaning up in the galley, my throat was sore. The truth was, the longer the voyage carried on, the more my desire to entertain waned. The tendency to play the clown seemed itself a mask, and now under the building stresses of the voyage, was peeling away. I wasn't sure I wanted to know what lurked underneath.

"I started aboard a clipper," he continues. "Eventually, word came of a gold strike in the still-untapped North. Immediately, I knew this was where I would go, though by the time I arrived in the Yukon territory, settling at the Forty Mile camp, the Klondike Rush was all but over. The conditions were no less brutal; incomprehensible to men of this day with their telephones and auto cars, their electric stoves and lights requiring little more than the turning of a knob or pressing down a pedal.

"A man doesn't appreciate comforts he hasn't earned. Quietly, they soften and disconnect him, turning luxuries into entitlements and men into weakened piles of mush. We slept on open decks without blankets while the Yukon winds swept in and bit us, and once on land, in holes dug in the snow like animals. I watched a man use a hunting knife to slice off the tops of his own frostbitten fingers to keep the gangrene from spreading. A week later he was back digging in the mines, cracking jokes about 'fingertip stew.'"

Telling how he rose from ignorant deckhand to captain, climbing through the ranks of cowardly incompetent men, unable to match his prowess, he breaks from his trance state, stands from his chair and begins tending to various chores around the cabin: tidying up, organizing charts, and papers at his desk. Finishing the chores, he picks up the tribal, wood-carved mask, puts it on and walks back to his chair.

As he stands facing me, donning the mask, my nerves again come undone. I'm certain he plans to first torture, then kill me, acting out some primal ritual while I'm bound to the wicker chair. The mask's mouth is carved into a demonic smile. The eyes are painted yellow with dark lashes protruding, like suns emitting rays. The nose is animalistic, the snout of a boar. If he puts an end to me, who will ever know what happened, or care? Maybe Reynolds and a few shipmates? Kate, if she hasn't completely dismissed me from her thoughts. The captain would be free to explain it away in whatever manner suited him: accident, suicide, unknown circumstances. Desperately, I scramble to think of things for which I need to repent, but none are forthcoming, probably because there are too many, but maybe because what requires repenting and what doesn't is muddy, and who would it benefit other than my own conscience? The whole effort feels forced and I drop it.

What has that spider in the ceiling crevice been feeding on? There must be others hidden on board, and without the usual supply of bugs, they've been forced to consume one another. A stream of random thoughts and images parade through my head like a moving picture show: a summer in childhood when a friend and I stole from the street vendors in Fell's Point, shoving fruit and vegetables into my pockets while the friend distracted the vendors with absurd questions;

Kate standing behind the soda shop counter, removing and neatly folding her apron, smoothing out her dress; the silver pocket watch taken by Renault's goons. I'd always assumed when the end arrived there'd be clarity, a peacefulness bathed in wisdom, but there are only hungry spiders and stolen vegetables.

A sharp tipped spear hangs on the wall near where the mask had been, and as I grow convinced that this will be his instrument of choice, my eyes well with tears. Just make it quick, I want to tell him. Spare me the torture and get it over with. He's no longer talking in my head. He stands for a minute peering at me through the mask, then sits down, placing both arms on the rests of his throne, a depraved king, banished forever to the sea.

I feel my arms move slightly, then my legs. Confident I can move freely again, I rise from the chair and nearly fall over. The winds have continued to grow and a storm is brewing. A book slides off the desk and lands on the floor with a thud. I grab the chair for support and without saying anything to the captain, turn and head for the door.

On deck the windrain engulfs me. I stagger forward into the storm's wrath, taking hold of a rail and then a stanchion to keep from being blown about the deck. I hear shouting and when I raise my head, the blurred forms of men through the rain are tying down the foremast sail, battening the hatches. The ocean swells are rising well above the deck and as the waves slam down on the ship, we take on water.

I'm barely moving. Exhausted, I think how easy it would be to let go of the rail, allowing myself to be swept into the waiting arms of the gale. The exhaustion is not like anything I've experienced; a draining of body and spirit that leaves me slap happy, drunk like. But I didn't endure whatever it is I've just endured to let myself be tossed overboard. Maintaining my grip, I continue pulling forward until I reach a hatch, then pull that far enough open to squeeze through. In my room, I'm too tired to bother shedding my soaked trousers before falling onto the cot and passing out.

* * *

The following morning in the galley, helping Mathiassen prepare a beef vegetable stew, shouts of "Land!" sound from the deck above. We join the rest of the crew now on the main deck peering out at a swath of land in the distance, starboard, maybe two miles away. After nothing but water for this long, the sight seems unreal, a mirage that will vanish in the morning mist at any moment, but instead, it grows, coming clearer into focus with a small range of green mountains sprouting from its interior.

The captain arrives, making his way past us to the tip of the bow with Kronen a few steps behind. I watch him carefully, searching for any discernible change, some acknowledgment that what I remember from the previous night actually occurred.

Through a pair of binoculars, he gazes out at the approaching island, and a minute later as he lowers them, he's in higher spirits than I've seen him since the night of our departure party. Wearing a satisfied grin, he hands the binoculars to Kronen.

As the island comes into view, hopes for a fantastical Eden, are squashed. Some of the crew groan in disappointment. A well-populated port is busy with an assortment of ships and fishing boats, unloading and taking on cargo. The roads, buildings and houses of an established town adjoining the port, sprawls into the hills. People are milling about the roads, pulling carts, engaged in their daily business. The captain informs us that when we dock, the crew are to remain on the ship while he and Kronen go ashore and conduct the business of obtaining the medicinal elixirs. This elicits an angry round of cursing and grumbling.

"Let us off the ship!" someone yells. What should've been a joyous occasion, an opportunity for the crew to renew their dimming spirits, has quickly become bitter and tense. Understanding the embers are hot, the captain moves quickly to quell the fire.

Climbing atop the bridge deck, he turns to address us: "Gentlemen, listen up now. I know it's been a long voyage and I well understand the frustration and disappointment, but I assure you I'm keeping you aboard the ship for your own good. This island is rife with contagious disease and a native population that looks on outsiders with hostile distrust. If the entire lot of us were to go, it would raise too much suspicion, putting everyone in danger. Remember that as captain I'm responsible for your safety. In lieu of the island, you'll have free reign of the ship and time to indulge whatever forms of recreation suit you. The beer kegs will of course be available in the galley if Mathiassen hasn't already finished them off. I ask only that you cause no physical damage to the ship— anyone who does so will be punished accordingly."

The crew responds with a hardy round of booing, but it's tempered, almost playful and the captain grins, confident that the fire if not put out is at least contained.

I assume I'm to remain on the ship with the rest, but as the captain passes me to walk the gangway, he says, "Dent, I'll need another hand while ashore, you'll come with us."
I'd meant to visit Reynolds early this morning to try and flesh out the previous night's strangeness, but I overslept by a few hours and had to immediately join Mathiassen in the galley. Before following captain Melfrane and Kronen over the gangway, I turn to him; "If we return tonight, I'll come by your room for a word."

I hesitate for a moment, but my reluctance is overwhelmed by a desire to set foot on solid ground and I cross the bridge, catching up to the two men now on the dock.

The island is a mishmash of people coming and going, most staying for a brief period to barter, buy and sell goods, to rest and replenish for a few days before resuming their voyages. A variety of races and nationalities mingle and blend easily at auctions and open markets, or to discuss some business venture or another. The place is rife with monkeys—little monkeys, milling about in the streets, markets, boarding houses, even restaurants. Somewhat like squirrels back home, but more prominent and without the skittishness. In fact, they mingle amongst the people with seemingly no fear whatsoever.

The captain is looking for his contact, someone familiar enough with the terrain to lead us into the island's interior where the magical elixirs await.

Having my feet on land brings a comfort and reassurance I'd forgotten existed, and I follow him and

Kronen down the town's main street until the captain stops, pulls a little notebook out of his satchel, checks an address and heads into a boarding house.

Kronen and I wait in the lobby while the captain approaches the desk to inquire about a guide who's name and address are written in his book. The buzz of activity is surprising with a steady flow of people coming and going. A door leads to an open patio area where men are smoking and talking. When a monkey runs right past us, out the front door, Kronen grins. "You must feel right at home Dent, what with all your little family members running around. Why don't you go find some bananas to bring to the reunion."

As his smug grin reaches across his face, I start to think of a retort, then let it go. My hatred for him is diminished. Being off the ship has lifted my mood, but even more, I don't want to be alone with the captain. If Kronen, along with his stupidity and shameless boot licking, can provide a kind of buffer, so be it. I have a strong sense the captain won't be casting any spells in his presence, certainly not in public.

"Where's he gone?" I ask, noticing the captain's no longer at the desk.

"Calm down," Kronen says, and a minute later he appears, followed by a man carrying a monkey on his shoulder.

"Mr. Hugo will be guiding us into the island's interior wilderness," the captain says.

Hugo is stockily built with a beard and glasses he repeatedly pushes back up as they slide down his nose. "Come on, we'll catch a ride to the interior," he says, barreling ahead through the front door. As the three of us follow, the little monkey turns on his shoulder, heeding us with caution.

Hugo hails a donkey-pulled cart driven by an islander. We lift ourselves into a canopied wagon bedded with hay, and start off toward the hills. He has the eccentric air of a scientist whose quirks are too many to count. "As you gentlemen can plainly see, the island has undergone a recent wave of growth and development, but the interior remains mostly uninhabited. Pierre and I take any opportunity to get away into the hills, isn't that right, Pierre?" he says, punctuating his words with a nervous high pitched laugh. From his shoulder perch, Pierre looks at me seated beside Hugo, then across at the captain and Kronen. His wide eyes and little face gleam with such intelligence, I half expect him to answer in English.

As the cart moves along, rocking lightly side to side, Hugo tells us he came to the island a decade ago doing work as a "cultural historian,"——work that apparently involves recording the customs and history of the islanders——and never left.

"Here, have some nuts." he says, pulling a bag of salted Macadamia nuts from his backpack and leans forward with the bag. Kronen and I readily take a handful each, while the captain refuses. He then holds the bag to his shoulder and Pierre reaches in for a helping.

"They're good, you ought to try some, Captain," I say, prodding him, expecting he'll shoot down the suggestion. Hugo again offers the bag and to my surprise the captain now takes a handful of nuts and begins popping them into his mouth one at a time. Seeing him eat is a welcome sight, evidence that he's but a man, after all.

From his satchel, he takes two maps, placing them in his lap, one set atop the other. The maps are roughly drawn and from what I can tell, he's combining them to create a more detailed and thorough picture. His dark trousers are tucked into his boots and the revolver is on his right hip, holstered to his brown leather belt. With an ink pen he makes little marks and notations on the maps. It's the first time I've seen him ashore and something about him is different, slightly ill at ease. Fretting and squinting over the maps, scratching at his beard, he looks almost uncomfortable.

"So Captain, what exactly is it we're looking for? Plants of some kind?" I ask.

"Huh?" he says, looking up distracted.

"These medical miracles we've come for, are they plants or leaves of some sort?"

"Plants? Yes, yes, plants."

"How will we know if we've found one, do you have pictures?"

"Yes, of course we have pictures," he says, going back to his maps.

"How do you know they'll work?"

"Not now, Dent, I'm busy" he says, without looking up.

"We ought to leave the worthless weasel right here on the island," Kronen says. "Let him swing in the trees with his monkey relatives."

"Scientifically speaking, sir, the four of us are all related to Pierre, here," Mr. Hugo says, giving Pierre an affectionate pet on the head.

For the first time the captain turns to acknowledge Kronen. "Try keeping your stupidity to yourself for a few minutes," he says, before diving back into his maps.

Kronen winces as though he's received an elbow to the ribs, then starts his muttering and cursing.

Apparently troubled by Mr. Hugo's suggestion, he takes a renewed interest in Pierre, peering at him with disdain.

"He's really quite friendly. Why don't you say hello?" Mr. Hugo says, taking Pierre from his shoulder to present to Kronen, but the monkey has other ideas. Unleashing a jarring, "Eighhh!" he scrambles free and hops right back up onto Hugo's shoulder.

"Well, maybe not today," Hugo concedes.

"He's obviously a good judge of character, I would've done exactly the same, Pierre," I say.

"You let that thing over here and I'll break its neck," Kronen says.

We continue winding up into the hills until the road is too rough and steep for the cart to travel any further. The foliage has grown gradually more dense and jungle like. Trees tower above us with enormous leaves that block the sun and spidery vines claw at the wagon and cart. The driver calls out "Haaa!" bringing the donkeys to a halt. We get out and stand to the side while the driver directs the animals to turn around. There's barely enough room and he has to keep slowly backing up, then go forward again to make a U-turn.

We pair up, the captain and I walking together with Kronen and Hugo maybe thirty yards behind. Red and green dragonflies the size of small birds buzz by my head. Enormous trees loom above, their spherical leaves shrouding us in a shade that's almost nocturnal. I'm city born and raised and the untamed forest unsettles me. Monkeys twice the size of Pierre sit on branches high above, tracking us with glowing eyes. I hear things scamper and rustle behind trees and into bushes. My mind starts to play tricks—what look like snakes in the near distance turn out to be fallen branches. The ship at least serves as a protective barrier against whatever lurks in the sea; out here there's none.

"This place has more plant species than I can count, Captain. How the hell will you find what you're looking for?"

"I'm not looking for plants, Dent, I'm looking for gold."

"Gold? I thought—"

"You thought I was looking for a plant that would cure the world of illness and terminal disease?"

"That's what you told us, that this Woodstock hired you to go in search of a medicine that would cure his disease. Why make up such a story? Why not—"

"The story isn't made up, not exactly. I'm just not searching for the thing Woodstock wanted me to find. Magical plants that cure deadly diseases?" He lets out his deep booming laugh. "That's a rich dream for poor fools. Even if such a thing existed, I'm not a goddamned botanist. I do know what gold looks like, and when I find it, hell if I want half the world knowing where it is. If I'd told that crew of sea rats what I was doing and let them off the ship, the entire island would know by now."

"I'm just another sea rat you hired to man the Phoenix. What makes you think I won't tell the crew?"

He's a step ahead of me as we walk in the deep shadows of the trees, but he slows until we're side by side, then gives me a stern glance. "Because, I've concluded you value your life enough not to do something which would so carelessly jeopardize it." He holds his gaze for another moment, making certain I've grasped his meaning, and then his entire demeanor shifts. He becomes collegial, slapping a hand down on my shoulder, grinning with amused satisfaction as I flinch at the touch. "Relax, my boy. Keep your mouth shut like I know you will, and there'll be quite a reward; wealth like you've never imagined."

He removes his meaty hand from my shoulder, increasing his pace until he's again a few strides ahead. It's not, I realize now, that he trusts or sees potential in me, but an unflinching assurance that I wouldn't dare try and impede him. He's purposefully surrounded himself with men who pose no threat to his authority: half-wits, drunks, clowns. . .

Feeling duped, I descend into a brooding, resentful, fog until I'm barely aware of the forest around me. The idea of finding my calling at sea under the captain's guidance is no less a pipe dream than the crew believing in an island full of naked nymphos.

We reach a small lake——more of a pond ,really——and the captain stops, retrieves his maps, and begins fretting over them while Mr. Hugo, Pierre, and Kronen catch up. He confers with Mr. Hugo over the geography, discussing how to proceed while Kronen and I stand back. I hear the captain's annoyed tone but can't make out what they're saying over the ecstatic screeches of parrots in the surrounding trees.

I wander off a ways, not too far, but enough to brood in privacy. I come to a spot where below the crotch of a tree, beside its wide trunk, lie several parrot feathers colored red, green, and blue. They're strikingly vibrant, not quite real looking, as though someone had taken a brush and freshly painted on the colors. When I pick one up off the ground and examine it, a memory of Kate momentarily lifts me out of the rain forest.

Both times I'd shown up at the soda shop with a gift for her, it hadn't gone well. She was the kind to be more impressed by thoughtfulness than expense, which should've worked in my favor since I had little expense to spare. She wanted to know the meaning behind the gift, why I'd chosen it, probably how it reminded me of her; but I had no such explanations. They were spur of the moment things I thought she would like: a cloche hat and a necklace of pearls. She wasn't dismissive, but her tempered reaction made it clear she wasn't altogether impressed.

She did express shock at the supposed cost of the necklace, though in reality I hadn't paid a cent for it. I'd been working at McSwain's one night when a woman, angry at the man who'd given it to her, basically dropped the necklace in my lap before storming out of the club. I figured telling Kate where it came from wouldn't have helped matters, and I let her go on believing I'd paid for it.

She was fond of birds, though, and had owned both a cockatoo and parakeet. When we went for walks, through a neighborhood or park, she'd stop and admire the city's variety of bird life, identifying species by their calls and plumage. Occasionally, she'd stand below a tree mimicking the calls of a Baltimore Oriole or black-throated warbler. Inevitably, someone walking by would stop and stare at her and I'd grow embarrassed, which she found very amusing.

Imagining she'll be quite pleased by them, I pick up the rest of the feathers and slip them into my pocket.

* * *

Re-joining the others, I hear the captain say: "I don't see anything on here. . . .How long is it?" while gesturing impatiently at a map.

"This part of the island has yet to be properly documented," Hugo responds with an admirable calm. "A year ago, I accompanied a cartographer into these parts but he was easily distracted and I never heard what became of his work. I did see one map and half of it was incorrect; guess work. Personally, I prefer it remain that way, to keep the mystery of it," he says, letting out his nervous laugh. He's younger than I first thought, the beard and quirky manner making him appear older. A strangely affable fellow, I decide.

"Just lead the way, Hugo," the captain says, and we head off again. It turns out, there's an unmapped river to the right of the little lake and Hugo has suggested we'll be able to follow it to our destination. In a couple of miles we reach the river and continue our trek along its banks, trudging through high wet grass. We trudge on for what feels like hours. "How much farther, Hugo?" the captain calls out over his shoulder; every mile or so. "Not so much longer now," Hugo repeats himself.

Just as I fear we're lost, we come to a place where the river forks and the surrounding banks grow almost circular, creating a wide, shallow pool of still water. The water's stillness evokes a peaceful solitude, and I can see down to the stones and pebbles which layer the river bed. Long slender fish swim languidly by in plain sight. The only noticeable sound comes from small rapids farther up, where the river forges ahead, beyond the pool.

Without his saying anything, I know this is the place the captain is looking for. He surveys the pool, squinting until his eyes settle on what appears to be a cave situated along the bank, on the far side of the pool. "Stay right here," he orders. He removes his revolver and holster, places them in the satchel with his maps and notebook, and secures it to his back.

He traces the bank around to the left where it steepens, uses his hands to stabilize himself against the mud of the bank, and descends into the pool. He wades through the waste-high water and in a moment, disappears into the cave.

Kronen, Hugo, Pierre, and I stand on the bank staring at the mouth of the cave in silent curiosity.

"Your captain seems to know exactly what he wants, not much hesitation in him," Hugo observes, frankly. "A bit impatient, but I'm sure a decent enough fellow on the whole," he adds before Kronen tells him to shut up.

"Back off, Kronen, Mr. Hugo here doesn't work aboard the Phoenix. He falls outside your jurisdiction of harassment."

Kronen turns toward me looking ready to exchange blows.

"Now now, gentleman, no need to be uncivil," Hugo rebukes us in a fatherly tone.

A few moments later the captain's booming voice echoes triumphantly from the cave.

"Ahh, it's here! A beautiful sight, indeed!"

We watch as he appears again outside the cave, wades through the lagoon and climbs the bank. "What is it? What's here?" Hugo asks, when the captain makes his way back to us.

"Gold, Mr. Hugo. A cave filled with beautiful shining gold."

"Where is it? Did you bring some with you?" Kronen says.

"No," the captain says, his voice dropping in sudden disappointment. "I'd been led to believe it would be placer gold—nuggets you can sweep from the ground and fill your pockets with like loose change. But it's vein gold, embedded in rock, requiring machinery and a whole operation to extract. First things first, though—son of a bitch, it's here," he says in a reverie, grinning at the prospect of his discovery.

"So there is gold after all. Others have come to the island looking for it, but as far as I know, without success. I hope, captain, whatever 'operation' you plan on running takes into careful consideration the surrounding habitat and cultural history of the islanders."

Hugo's words pull the captain out of his reverie and he shoots him a look that makes his disdain for the man clear.

My near-complete lack of excitement over the discovery surprises me. I've no desire even to see what it looks like: gold in its natural state. The humid tropical heat is relentless. I'm tired, and my feet throb and burn from all of the walking.

Kronen is worse off than I am. As we walked in the high grass along the bank, he stumbled twice, the second time nearly falling down the bank into the river. His florid cheeks puff with exhaustion and his nostrils flare like a bull's.

"Will we be heading back now, Captain?" I ask. "It's getting late and we haven't eaten anything besides a few nuts."

"For God's sake, show some fortitude. You want mama to cook you a warm meal and tuck you under the sheets? It's time you grew a pair, Dent," he says. Then adds, "We'll be off shortly," as he makes more notations on his maps.

His words agitate my insides, awakening the clown. "Hunger, combined with exhaustion and poor judgment, I'm sure has led to countless deaths, Captain. Or we can just stay here all night ringing the dinner bell so the snakes and panthers know exactly where to find us."

We retrace our steps through the high grass, above the river. After maybe two miles, at Mr. Hugo's suggestion, we alter our route to take a shortcut through the dense forest. Clearing a path through the encroaching brush, we swat back vines and branches that grab at us like slender arms. The exertion this requires and a growing certainty that snakes are slithering unseen at my feet, fill me with dread. The exhilaration I'd felt upon first setting foot on the island is a distant memory and I fear we'll never make it back to the ship.

"What's the point of this?" I say, to no one in particular. A few minutes later, the thick brush opens abruptly into a clearing and what appears to have been a small, native settlement, long abandoned. The dilapidated remains of log-built huts, their mud-insulated roofs, and walls capsized by time and the elements populate the clearing. In the middle of the clearing a fire pit is surrounded on four sides by totems. A fifth, shorter, more intricately designed totem is positioned next to the pit, between the other four.

"I thought before returning, you gentlemen might want to experience some of the island's historical relics," Hugo says, giving an overview of the living conditions and customs of the early islanders.

The captain, having no time for Hugo's history lesson, makes a beeline for the totems, stopping a few feet before the nearest one to appraise it. I think of the indigenous artifacts in his cabin—the masks and spear—can almost hear him calculating its value, devising a way to add it to his collection. Hugo, Pierre, Kronen and I follow, stopping at the near side of the fire pit.

"Ah, I see the totems have gained your interest, and rightfully so," Mr. Hugo says, smiling, pleased by the opportunity to act as tour guide. "You'll notice, there are four totems, representing each of the geographical directions: north, south, east, west. The fifth, smaller one, is significant in that it indicates both the heavens above, and the spiritual underworld which the early tribes believed existed far below the earth's surface. A richly imagined world of phantoms and supernatural beings."

"Spiritual underworld," Kronen scoffs. "The heathens are paying their dues in hell."

"That's certainly one perspective," Mr. Hugo retorts.

Pierre, who's been quiet, hops down from his master's shoulder and scours the area for nuts and insects to eat.

The open clearing has revealed the sky, bathing us in the orange glow of early dusk. The fading light against the trees creates a pleasant luminous gleam. It's cooler, and aside from the occasional bird call, quiet. I stand very still, my boots planted in the earth, letting insects crawl about my arms and face until I feel myself merging with the forest. Fearing I'm about to morph into a tree or patch of grass, I shudder and with a sudden strike, slap my forearm, killing a mosquito.

The captain has moved to inspect the smaller totem that stands between the others. "I like this one very much," he says, reaching his hand out to caress it. "I believe it will fetch an impressive price."

"With due respect, Captain, the totems are a part of the island's heritage and not for sale. Certainly, they're not yours to sell," Hugo says, striding over to confront the captain. As though sensing his uneasiness, Pierre interrupts his hunt, comes bounding over from one of the huts, and hops back up onto Hugo's shoulder.

The captain, appearing to ignore or not notice him, makes no move to turn away from the totem. Then he says, "And who exactly will stop me from doing so, Mr. Hugo?"

An anxiousness sprouts up in the pit of my empty stomach.

"They're protected by legal mandate enacted by the island's governing body. I won't hesitate to tell the authorities."

Captain Melfrane turns to face Mr. Hugo and the two men begin to argue, their voices rising as they struggle to be heard over the other. The argument is a brief one. The captain does not suffer insubordination kindly, no matter whether it involves an actual subordinate. Having heard enough, he calmly removes the revolver from its holster and fires a shot. Hugo, clutches at his chest and drops silently to his knees while Pierre let's out a horrific, human like scream. Still screeching, he scrambles off across the clearing, disappearing into the brush.

"Why?" is all I can muster, hurrying to tend to Mr. Hugo, now on his back, unconscious. I squat over him, take a rag from my pocket and try for a minute to stem the bleeding but Mr. Hugo is gone.

"We'll bury him in the pit," I hear the captain say from behind, his voice steady, void of emotion.

"Oh will we? And what if I don't?" I say, standing and turning to face him.

"Then there's plenty of room for two graves, Dent," he says, removing the satchel from his back and laying it in the grass. Kronen hasn't moved since the gunshot and his red, overheated face has gone ashen. "Did you have to kill him, Captain?" he says, his voice shaking.

I'm suffocating, my breaths growing short and unsteady until it's as if I've forgotten how to breathe and have to force the air in and out. A pathogen has settled deep inside my chest and I need to cough it up before it does more damage.

But what really can I do? I know I'm no match for this man who half the time hardly seems a man at all. Who dismisses starvation like an inconvenient head wind; who's taught himself not to feel pain and subordinates men with the steel grip of his glare. From his satchel he removes a small shovel, probably initially intended to dig for gold, but which he now thrusts into the side of the pit, breaking up and dislodging the mud caked earth. Kronen and I scoop up the crumbling dirt with our hands and forearms and drop it on top of Hugo who we've laid face up in the pit, his arms folded about his chest like someone who's caught cold, or is overseeing the work of others. They don't quite cover the bloody wound. I instruct myself not to look at his

face, then disobey my own instruction, observing that his
eyes are thankfully closed, and his slightly open mouth
is frozen into the beginning of a smile. His peaceful
expression slightly eases my angst and I wonder if he's
already joined the spirits in the underworld.

As we bend and rise, covering Mr. Hugo with
clumps of red soil, Kronen resumes his muttering,
interspersed with low whimpering noises. Soon after Mr.
Hugo is no longer visible, a giant earthworm — which
I at first judge to be a snake—rears up from beneath a
pile of freshly dug dirt and squirms frantically about.
The thing is two feet long and both Kronen and I halt
our work and take a few steps back. Moments later, the
backside of a shovel crashes down on the worm's head,
rendering it lifeless in the dirt, followed by the captain's
steady voice: "Keep your wits about you, men; it'll be
dark soon. Let's hurry this up."

The nonchalance is what unnerves me—killing
Mr. Hugo without a twitch of hesitation, as though
exterminating an insect. About time I grew a pair? Be
careful what you wish for, captain. Somewhere down
there, I've already got a pair and when I finally put
them to use, I'll be coming for you, mighty king, doing
everything in my power to expel your contaminated
soul from the throne.

These are my brave thoughts as the captain
orders me and Kronen to drop a final blanket of dirt
atop poor Mr. Hugo, then levels and smooths over the
earth with the back of his shovel.

Thoughts mean little. Without conviction, they
come and go like the rolling tide and I still don't know
what I'll do, or how. Perhaps his meager estimate of my
backbone will prove correct. For now, it requires all my

resolve to continue putting one foot in front of the other until we reach the ship.

Chapter 4

Back on board, I move around the ship wearing a mask of calm normality, but it only seems to set me further on edge. Less than two days after our return, I'm standing in the galley, staring absently at the oven, ignoring Mathiassen's instructions regarding that evening's dinner preparation.

"Dent, have you heard a word I've said?" He walks over and examines me with concerned curiosity. "You don't look so well; like you've seen a ghost."

"How do you know him, Mathiassen? A storm is engulfing the ship and I don't want to die on board," I say, in an anguished voice, not much louder than a whisper.

"How do I know, who?"

"The captain, the captain."

Sensing my desperation, Mathiassen grabs his bottle of Cabernet Sauvignon around the neck and sits in the single chair we keep in the galley, against the wall between the ovens. He takes a swig and then begins: "First off, my real name is Woodstock, son of Halverton Woodstock, owner of this ship and sponsor of this voyage. Melfrane, hearing—perhaps through one of the notices placed in newspapers—that my father was in the market for someone to captain the Phoenix on its expedition, quickly made himself acquainted. He met my father at a prominent—and I might add,very pretentious—social club and soon after, was making regular visits to the estate, west of Baltimore. He ingratiated himself to my sickly father until he wouldn't have thought of hiring anyone else for the job. As Melfrane somewhat explained the night before we pulled up anchor, my father's health was quickly failing and eccentric that he was, decided he would pursue these so called medicinal elixirs he'd read about in one of several absurd publications. They were little more than the fantastical nonsense you see peddled on street corners with stories claiming proof of one-eyed space creatures and talking horses."

"'Eccentric that he was.'"

"Yes, he passed well before we went to sea."

"He really believed that stuff?"

"He didn't subscribe to standard medicine; didn't much subscribe to standard anything. When I was a child he hosted seances at the estate and when confronted with a difficult decision, visited palm and tarot readers. And by this time, he'd grown desperate. What did he have to lose?

"Anyway, Melfrane ingratiated himself to more than just my father. He took a great interest in my charming Isabel. Mind you, she had never been anything approaching faithful. Disgusted with my drinking and own indiscretions, she'd had several affairs by that time. My recent dismissal from the university for 'excessive consumption and unprofessional conduct' left her furious with me and we bickered constantly. When I found out about Melfrane though, I couldn't let it go. I told myself what I always did—that she meant nothing and the affair even less, but this was different. His presumptuous arrogance—the way he practically flaunted the affair in my face—all the while taking advantage of a dying old man. I'd never much gotten on with my father, but that was little consolation.

"It was a cold night, the kind that turns the breath to frosted clouds before it's left your mouth. The frozen grass crunched beneath my feet. In a state of filthy drunkenness with which you've become quite familiar, I stumbled upon the two of them carrying on in the old barn located on the estate. The upper portion of the barn had been converted into a spacious guest lodging and I could see them upstairs through a window embracing. I flew into an uncontrollable rage, shaking as though I'd caught pneumonia. I went to a near shed, found a can of gasoline, carried it back and poured it around the perimeter of the barn until it was empty. I wasn't thinking about what I was doing, I was under a spell, at the complete mercy of my rage. I lit a match and watched it go up. The velocity with which the fire caught and grew was astounding; in no more than a minute the entire barn was engulfed. I stood there watching, hypnotized as the rising flames joined hands and danced. The scorching heat on my face and panicked neighing of horses in an adjacent stable, brought me back to what was happening. In a frenzy I circled the barn looking for a way in—at least to try and

The Captian's Spell

save my Isabel—but it was too late. Of course Melfrane escaped mostly unscathed."

He's about to take another swig from the bottle, stops, places it on the floor beside the chair and stares at the oven. He's as broken as a man can be; not even desiring to be repaired, just waiting out the time till he's succeeded in obliterating himself.

We remain in silence a minute, him in the chair, me standing ten feet away just beyond the ovens.

"But if you're father had already died, how did Melfrane gain control of the ship?"

Pulled out of his reverie, Mathiassen looks at me for a few seconds, then rubs the skin on his forehead. "As reparation for setting the fire, he wanted my father's inheritance, especially the Phoenix. He threatened to turn me into the authorities if I didn't oblige. My father's estate was going to take months or more to settle and fearing I'd flee, or that the police would apprehend me before the assets could be transferred, he decided to drag me to sea, keeping me prisoner aboard my father's ship while things settled back home."

"You thought the captain believed the story about disease-curing plants?"

Mathiassen considers it. "My father was quite a salesman and once he convinced himself of something would promote it relentlessly. I think the more they spoke about it, the more Melfrane grew enamored of the idea. A discovery of that magnitude would make my father's assets seem like driftwood, while establishing Melfrane as the legend he clearly believes himself to be. It was the kind of proposition to make a man like him salivate."

"It wasn't magic plants making him salivate, it was gold."

"What?"

I tell him about the island and Mr. Hugo's murder.

"I can't say I'm surprised by it," he says, finally. "He's right to think I'd poison him, to have me bring his meals to his cabin and sample them while he watches. If I'd any spine at all, I'd have found a way to end him already, but it seems I'm every bit invertebrate as a jellyfish or shrimp."

At this, he stares past me, across the galley, drifting off into some dark recess of his mind.

* * *

That evening after dinner, I meet with Reynolds in his cabin. The Phoenix remains anchored off the island, but word has spread amongst the crew that the captain will address us in the morning, advising of changes to our itinerary and a time table for the voyage home. I'm no longer convinced there will be such a voyage.

"You don't look well," Reynolds says, seated on his cot.

Too on edge to sit at the little desk, I first stand by the door, then walk about the little room, having to stop and turn around every few steps.

"You need to calm down," Reynolds says, reaching over and pulling open a desk drawer. He takes out a bottle of rum, pours me half a glass and places it on the desk. "Here, this'll help."

"I didn't know you drank."

"Not like these drunks who have it with breakfast every morning, but it does serve a purpose on occasion."

I pick up the glass, down it and put it back on the desk. For a moment my face and eyes burn, then a pleasant warmth descends into my chest and stomach.

"He's a murderer," I blurt out. "We need to stop him before its too late."

"Murderer?"

"Yes, on the island he shot and killed a man named Hugo. Shot him in cold blood like it was nothing, right in front of me and Kronen."

"Why?"

"Because he dared disagree with him. This whole time the captain's been looking for gold and he found it on the island. He wants it for himself and this Hugo was a kind of guardian of the island's history who had no intention of keeping his little secret. When the captain made it clear he intended to remove a historical artifact and sell it, the two started to argue and a minute later Mr. Hugo was dead."

Reynolds narrows his eyes into a piercing squint, his face twisting in disgust. "So it was gold. I knew his story about Woodstock and miracle plants was a crock, but I couldn't figure out what he was up to."

"Except there really is a Halverton Woodstock, at least there was."

I tell him about Mathiassen/Woodstock and his history with the captain. When I'm done, Reynolds rubs his temples and pours himself a glass of rum. I want to tell him about my meeting with the captain the night before we found the island, but don't entirely believe it myself, suspecting it was a kind of trick or illusion performed under hypnosis. I certainly wouldn't have believed it if someone else tried to tell me it happened to them.

"What should we do?"

Reynolds gives a perplexed look and thinks about it. "We should wait to hear what he says tomorrow morning. We'll know better then, his intentions—how long he plans to keep us hostage aboard this cursed vessel."

"Hostage? Reynolds, I wish you wouldn't talk like that."

"How should I talk then? We're stuck here at the mercy of his whims and sinister schemes."

"Can you do something with your voodoo?"

Reynolds laughs scornfully. "That was a quick conversion, Dent. I didn't even have to light candles or do a spirit dance," he says.

"Let's just say I've witnessed a few things recently that make it easier to swallow. And what else can we do? He seems to hold all of the cards."

"Not all. There's over twenty men on the ship and none that I know of are in his corner, except Kronen."

"I think even Kronen is having doubts after seeing Mr. Hugo shot down like a dog. He may be the only one left the captain trusts; I wonder if we could recruit him to find out first what the captain's planning, then help overtake him," I say, sitting down at the little desk.

"Why depend on that scoundrel? The captain enlists you to inform on the crew, then brings you with him onto the island. He's taken quite an interest in you; you could use your own sway to find out what he has in store."

"No," I say, shaking my head and looking at the floor. "Whatever appeal I held was buried on the island. After letting him know what I thought of his execution of Mr. Hugo, his attitude changed. As we made our way out of the forest, he insisted I walk ahead. 'Keep in front, Dent, where I can see you. No more than ten paces in front of me,' he ordered. I was sure he'd shoot me in the back and kept trying to increase my distance a little at a time so he wouldn't notice. But each time I gained a couple of feet, he'd yell at me to slow down. I still can't believe I made it back alive.

"Do you have anything besides a bag of rocks? A doll we can poke needles into, some kind of spell we can put on him?"

"You made it back, didn't you?" Reynolds says, offended.

"I don't think rocks had much to do with it."

"So what makes you believe a spell will do anything?"

"I don't know, I'm grasping at straws here, Reynolds."

"I'm a carpenter and merchant marine, not a medicine man. I don't have any spells."

I sigh and grab the back of my neck. "It feels like we're already sinking, maybe we could make one up."

"For a conjuring to work, all doubt must be erased. You must see and believe in it like I see my hand right now," he says, raising his left hand and passing it slowly in front of his face. "And that would make it near impossible where you're concerned."

"If he addresses the crew tomorrow morning on the main deck, we can try overtaking him, then. We'll need the help of the crew, at least some of them, and then we'll have to be quick about it, before he has time to suspect anything."

"You're serious," Reynolds says, looking me over like someone he's never seen just entered the room.

"Dead serious."

"Just overpower the captain there on the deck?"

"There's strength in numbers—you said yourself none of the crew is in his corner. If enough men join us, what can he do?"

"He can blast a hole through you with that revolver he wears on his belt the way other men wear shoes and socks."

"He can't shoot all of us."

"Just because the crew hates him doesn't mean they'll rise in mutiny. Their greatest worry is when and where their next drink's coming. How many men will he shoot before he's taken down?"

Reynolds's words rattle me, but I persist."You under-sell them. Once they learn what he's up to, that he plans to keep them on board against their will and their lives are in danger, they just might."

Reynolds looks at me with puzzled caution.

"I really wish you'd stop looking at me that way."

"What way is that?"

"Like you've never seen me before, like I'm an imposter."

"Well, it almost seems like you went to the island, and someone else came back."

"I'd never seen anyone murdered in cold blood before, and now the picture of it won't go away. It's funny, all this time my disgust was aimed at Kronen. Now that I know what the captain is, my hatred for the first mate seems petty."

But this wasn't the half of it. Since returning from the island two nights before, I couldn't sleep or think of anything other than stopping the captain while protecting myself from his murderous wrath.

I spent hours locked in my room and had taken to barricading the door by propping a chair on two legs against it, along with a desk. With a piece of string, I'd tied together several pieces of silverware taken from the galley and hung them around the doorknob so they'd alert me to the door's slightest movement. When I did venture from my room, it was usually to tend to my duties helping Mathiassen in the galley, and if I came across any of the crew, I immediately grew suspicious, trying to gauge which of them were working as the captain's informants; the same men who a few days before hadn't given me any reason to believe they were doing anything other than their jobs.

At night, laying sleepless on my cot, I'd stare at the ceiling planks, reliving the incidents from the island. At first I'd believed the captain had killed Mr. Hugo because of their disagreement over the totem, but the more I considered it, the more I was convinced he'd never intended to let Mr. Hugo out of the forest alive. Not wanting him to know about the gold, the totem had just been a convenient excuse to shoot him. The captain after all wasn't a man who left things to chance.

My head reeled with violent fantasies. In one, I swiped the gun out of his side holster, shot him in the chest at point blank range, then stood over him, watching as he writhed in pain on the ground. In another, I sneaked into his cabin and taking the tribal spear from the wall, waited for him to return from his evening rounds. As he came through the cabin door, I plunged the spear into his gut. I didn't really mean to kill him, I assured myself; just to overtake him and keep him locked in the brig until we arrived safely home.

But I had no idea how. I've never been good with strategy or logistics; I only knew what needed to be done and that the captain was no doubt this very moment in his quarters, making calculations, plotting his deviant course. I was desperately hoping Reynolds could help come up with a plan.

I stand from the chair and pace the room again.

"You need to calm yourself before you do something rash."

"We're going to calmly end up at the bottom of the ocean if we don't do something, Reynolds!"

"Lower your voice; sound carries easily through these old planks. We need to wait for a sign."

"I'm done waiting anymore. He'll think nothing of shooting anyone he believes threatens his gold, and honestly, he believes everyone is a threat."

Still seated on the cot, Reynolds hunches over with his elbows on his knees, bows his head and places two fingers from each hand on his temples. He remains this way for more than a minute, long enough that I begin to think he's actually trying to conjure up some black magic. Finally he looks up. "If we cause a distraction while he's addressing the crew, we may be able to catch him off his guard. Something to spark his rage while he's making his speech . . ."

* * *

Early the next morning we're gathered about the main deck, between the pilothouse and bow, awaiting the captain to advise us of our fate. He's not yet arrived and I think how it's just like him to keep us in limbo, one more way to demonstrate his authority over us.

It is a gray morning, and clouds race quickly through the sky and past the ship as if fleeing to safer ground. Having absorbed the grayness of the sky, the ocean is opaque and a steady wind roils its surface, which bodes well for our plan.

As is his custom when addressing the crew, we've determined the captain will ascend from the hatch leading to his quarters, then make his way in front of the pilothouse and bridge deck while the crew gathers about him in a kind of semicircle. Once he's positioned, we will position ourselves in kind. Don and Dale will be on either side of him, Reynolds will stay next to Kronen, ready to restrain him when or if he interferes, and I will be in the very back, where I now stand, a few feet behind the group, closest to the bow. As we wait, I look around, checking to see if anyone is missing. Everyone is properly situated. The only one not accounted for is Mathiassen/Woodstock, whom I'd already assumed would be passed out from a night of trying to drink himself into oblivion.

Finally, the hatch opens as though by its own volition and out rises the captain, slow and dreamlike in the vague grayness of the morning. Closing the hatch, he takes a moment to look about, noting the weather and condition of the ship, his critical eye searching for anything amiss. Seemingly satisfied, he strides toward the gathering of men who part like the Red Sea for Moses—then, once reaching the pilothouse, turns and places his hands on hips.

As he begins speaking, I remove from under my shirt the kite Reynolds helped me construct the previous night: a sawed off closet door handle used as a spool for string tied at its end with an assortment of garment fragments cut from mine and Reynolds' clothing. A healthy wind ripples the foremast sail, blowing port side to starboard. Keeping at the edge of the semicircle, I move slowly to port side, spool in one hand, rags in the other. I let out the string, keeping hold of the kite rags until I think there's enough to quickly raise them to a good height, then let go. As if privy to our plan and in full agreement with it, the rags shoot immediately skyward over the heads of the crew, then are pulled across the deck and over the starboard side of the hull. Several men turn to look, as does the captain, who stares at it in confused silence, appearing caught off guard for the first time since I've known him.

"Look at your kite, Captain! Better catch it before it flies away!" I yell.

Don and Dale both move in to take hold of him, but quick as a cat and seemingly all in one motion, he unholsters the revolver, steps forward, yanks Henry out of the front of the group and rests the steel barrel against his head. "Back off of me!" he yells, pulling frail Henry roughly against him as a shield.

Don and Dale move slowly away as do the rest of the crew, some of them raising their hands above their heads in submission. Reynolds, who has taken hold of Kronen, grabbing him from behind by the arms, now releases him.

"Keep your monkey hands off me!" Kronen yells, shaking free of his grip. I toss the spool on the deck and the kite continues to climb and whip in the wind, the white rags waving above the ship like a flag of surrender.

I look about for help from another vessel or from someone on the island, but we are ported well away from other ships, and it's impossible for anyone on the island to see what's happening on board. What an ill conceived mess of a plan! Grasping for something to sway circumstances in our favor, I start pleading for occurrences I don't actually believe in: interference from a higher power; Henry mustering up the strength and courage to overtake the captain.

His back against the pilothouse bridge and his gun on Henry, the captain edges toward starboard.

"Keep back now. Any man who defies me pays with his life!" he says, clutching Henry tight with one arm. Each time he moves, Henry's feet lift a few inches off the deck and his legs and arms dangle with the limp weight of a doll. His wide eyes are begging for someone to end his misery.

"I want Kronen to lower the starboard gangway!" orders the captain.

He continues edging along, sidestepping like a crab until he reaches the end of the bridge. He looks about smiling, and I realize he's actually savoring this chaos. He takes one more step, turning to port side, and then, from around the corner of the bridge, comes a long silver blade and the thrust of an arm.

Missing Henry by mere inches, the blade plunges unimpeded into the captain's lower chest. It goes in deep, sinking in until much of the blade is hidden inside him. He releases Henry who scampers away, and crouches behind a few of the crew huddled at the bow.

"Burn in hell miserable demon!" Mathiassen shouts, releasing the blade, which I now recognize as the large butcher's cleaver hanging all this time unused on the galley wall. He steps back, leaving the cleaver to protrude by itself from the captain's flesh. The captain, making no move to pull it out, raises the revolver, takes careful aim and shoots Mathiassen through the neck.

He falls to the deck clutching at his throat, and again the captain takes aim, shooting him dead where he lays.

With Mathiassen out of the way, he turns suddenly toward the bow where most of us have gathered, seeking refuge in numbers. Men gasp and moan in horror as the captain stands with the cleaver protruding from his chest like an unnatural appendage. Holstering the revolver, he looks down at the knife and his bloodied white linen shirt, as though noticing them for the first time, then with both hands, in a slow and steady motion, pulls forth the blade. He does this without so much as a wince or moan escaping his lips pursed tight in a bitter smile, and I recall his coming of age story, teaching himself to transcend pain, to appreciate it even. Could it be he's taking pleasure in his wound? No, it isn't possible, I decide, not in any kind of sane manner.

With the cleaver dislodged, the blood hemorrhages, cascading out of the wound, down his black trousers. He makes a slight but sudden movement forward, and when several men call out in fearful protest, he laughs quietly to himself, pleased that even amid this deathly chaos and rebellion, he continues to hold sway over them. Moving again, this time away from us, he steps haphazardly, zigzagging his way toward starboard, stumbles, then regains his balance. Reaching the edge of the ship, with one arm he grabs hold of the steel rail for support, and with the other tosses the cleaver overboard. He turns and faces us again, supporting himself against the bulwark and smiling as if everything were going exactly to plan. "You see that, gentlemen. That's how you carry out your duty; with diligence and dedication. This work requires resolve."

At that he reaches for his holster.

"Ahhh!" "Watch it! "Look out!" men yell, ducking and moving behind stanchions and the forecastle steps for cover.

But he just sinks slowly down with his back pressed against the bulwark and collapses on deck.

For several moments, not believing it possible the captain has met his end, nobody moves. No one could survive such a gruesome injury and loss of blood, and yet, I half expect him to rise from the deck, and with his derisive laugh, scold us for ever thinking he was gone.

Finally, curiosity compels several of us to begin moving toward him and we cross the deck planks with slow cautious strides, readying ourselves in the event he suddenly rouses from his sleep. Five feet away, we stop and stand, looking down on him. The body is impossibly limp and lifeless, the face drained of blood, is ghostly white. The eyes, still open, stare unseeingly up at the grey windswept clouds, while his sprawled legs lay open with the feet splayed out. The right arm's at his side, tucked against the hull and the left crosses his chest, covering most of the bloody gash, as though intent on maintaining an appearance of strength and respectability.

"What should we do with him?" someone asks.

"There's body bags in the utility room next to the brig," I hear Reynolds' voice say, and look over to see he's standing beside me. "We'll need two of them."

Still stunned and struggling to comprehend what's happened, the entire crew mills aimlessly about the deck, some speaking in low murmurs, others just shaking their heads. Nobody seems to know what to do next. Then a scuffle breaks out followed by shouting.

"Get off me you clumsy oaf!" I hear Dale yell.

"I didn't touch you, ass head!" Don yells back.

"The hell you didn't."

They start pushing, then clasp each other about the upper arms and neck, wrestling across the deck in an awkward dance of flailing arms and kicking legs that mostly miss their targets. A few of the crew rush over to untangle them and keep them apart for a few minutes while they calm down. It's a dance we're all quite familiar with by now and it has the unintended effect of restoring some normalcy to the situation.

As though jarred out of a collective haze, the crew return to their routines. Men begin cranking the anchor wheel, pulling the chain cable and anchor back into the ship, while the helmsman climbs the bridge and takes his position in the pilothouse. Crispen and the firemen head below to resume their work in the engine and boiler rooms. One of the mates returns with the bags and several of us load Mathiassen/Woodstock and then the captain into their respective bags. We're all eager to get as far away from this cursed island as fast as we can, and soon the ship is in motion, coursing northeast over the Caribbean Sea.

A mile out, we weigh the captain's bag down with chains, tie it with rope and drop the body overboard into the ocean.

"And may he always remain down there," someone says.

When the mates move to repeat the procedure with Mathiassen/Woodstock, I stop them. I can't help believe if we drop the bodies in the same spot, they'll continue to battle upon the ocean for eternity.

"Let's wait a bit and put a good distance between the two," I say, as they start to lift him off the deck. "I think Mathiassen at least, would prefer it that way."

A few hours later we hoist up Mathiassen and drop him into the sea. "A hero and a damn fine cook," I say.

The men "Aye," and nod, passing around a bottle of whiskey toasting Mathiassen/Woodstock.

* * *

One night, five days into the journey home, something compels me to rise from my cot, head up the companion way to the main deck and down the hatch leading to the captain's quarters. For some minutes, I just stand outside the door listening, as though I'll soon hear him pacing about the cabin or maybe rustling papers at his desk.

When I turn the doorknob, surprisingly, it's unlocked. Inside, I light the oil lamp on his desk and then another brighter one which stands against the wall, closer to the door. I'm looking for something, though I've no idea what. Perusing the charts, papers and notebooks on his desk, I find among other things, the two maps of the island and the notebook with Mr. Hugo's information. I rummage through a few of the drawers finding several compasses, binoculars and other items which hold no particular interest.

Sitting at his desk chair, I gaze up at the collection of tribal artifacts hanging on the back wall which now include the totem he took from the island. My eyes settle on the mask he wore during our meeting when I was frozen to the chair. I go to the wall, take the mask from the nail on which it hangs and as I put it on, become aware of his scent still permeating the room; a mixture of cherry tobacco, whiskey and a distinct wooded musk. I cross the cabin to the burgundy, makeshift throne, and donning the mask, sit down in it. I'm not sure what I expect to accomplish by this gesture. Perhaps, for a few moments, I'll know what it is to hold and wear authority with a natural ease. Perhaps the secrets of hypnotic telepathy and second sight will be revealed. I place my forearms on the armrests inlaid with stones, lean against the over sized back, and planting my boots firmly on the floor, stare intently ahead at the door.

* * *

The voyage back to Baltimore is slow and the crew strangely subdued. I wonder if like me, they sense the captain has not entirely left the ship. Not that I expect to see his ghost making the evening rounds, but his presence unmistakably lingers on board so that at times, cleaning the main deck or forecastle, I'll suddenly stop and turn aft, expecting to see him standing atop the poop deck, a statue of nobility, overseeing the work of his underlings.

After dinner one evening with the setting sun painting the sky a pleasant orange purple, I take my guitar and head up to the weather deck. Much of the crew are about, smoking, playing cards, talking. Leaning against a bulwark, I play "Wellerman," "What Shall We Do with the Drunken Sailor," and "Spanish Ladies" After a few minutes, several men join in and sing along.

Chapter 5

The night we ported in Baltimore, the crew fled like a flock of pigeons evading an oncoming streetcar, practically tripping over themselves to get off the ship before the gangway had even gone down. I resumed residence at my old flat, doing little besides sleep and eat. We had never been paid and after a few weeks I had to find work. I found it at a print shop off Roberson Street. Ten to twelve hour days, returning home for a meal, then getting up the next morning to do it all over again. My hands and clothing were constantly stained with a black ink that wouldn't completely wash out, so even on my days off, I was unable to escape the shop with its carbon dyes and harsh resin odors.

Since the Phoenix's return voyage, I'd begun thinking more and more of Kate. I didn't feel ready to meet in person and talk, but still I longed to see her and so from a distance would stake out the soda

shop, or her house, hoping to get a glimpse of her. I kept the parrot feathers tucked in my pocket in case I had a spontaneous impulse to approach. It was during one of these spying sessions (there's really not a more delicate way to describe what I was doing) that I saw her walk out of the soda shop with her new beau—a large, husky fellow, well dressed with a gray twill flat cap and burgundy scarf. As they descended the shop steps smiling, he placed a husky arm around her shoulder and I recoiled in disgust before nearly stepping out from behind the bus stand I was using as a blind, and yelling at him to keep
his fat hands to himself.

Conveniently, I'd avoided thoughts of her taking up with somebody else and the realization left me burning with resentment. As they crossed the street and walked toward me, I stood very straight and still behind the stand like an officer at attention, and when they passed I followed, keeping at a good distance, ready to duck into an alley or behind a pedestrian in case they suddenly stopped or looked back. I'd no idea what I would do, but I'd been overtaken by an attitude so foreign to my nature I imagined this was what people meant when speaking of someone "possessed." I didn't seem to be acting entirely of my own volition.

Though I'd been the one to end the affair, I felt betrayed, angry she hadn't allowed for the possibility of reconciliation. I couldn't stop thinking how I'd endured a month on a ship captained by a madman, brought her back exotic feathers from the Caribbean, only to find she'd taken up with this pretentious galoot.

Stirred by fury and this unchecked mania, I became a night prowler, tracking Kate and her husky gorilla man at every opportunity. I tailed them to the theater, sitting ten rows behind as they laughed and yelled at a moving picture starring Groucho Marx. Before the show ended, I slipped out of my seat and went outside to stand on the corner. Coat collar up, cap pulled down, I leaned against a lamppost waiting for them to exit the theater and then, as they turned down the avenue, I followed. The care free manner in which they strolled along, casually touching the other's arm while making a point, or throwing their heads back to laugh, infuriated me, seemed purposefully disrespectful, as if they should have somehow known I might be there watching.

"Oh Harrison," she said, tugging affectionately on his coat sleeve, "don't be such a meany,"

"Harrison," I repeated to myself. What an absurd, pretentious name. She had never acted this way with me, with this uninhibited lightness and casual display of affection on public streets. Why not? I wondered, growing more bitter. What kind of vile unsavory tricks was he using to seduce her? He must've been lying through his nose, promising marriage and the comforts of life in a big gated house, outside the city, which he would never deliver on. Harrison, with his unscathed hands and upper crust attire looked like he'd never done a hard day's work in his life.

I wanted to frighten them, to fill them with the same terror I'd experienced aboard the ship and on the island, and in this desire, felt myself taking on the qualities of a predator. As I followed them down a quiet side street, my thoughts became volatile enough that I feared what I might do. Full of wretchedness and self-disgust, I dodged into an adjoining alley and stood for several minutes in the darkness, leaning against the side of a building with my eyes closed. Finally, I turned back in the opposite direction looking for a street car home.

I'd begun to have trouble sleeping. The worst of it being when I'd dream of the voice—resonant and deep, exactly as I'd heard it on the ship and in my head during our meeting in his quarters. He'd be going on eloquently about the brutality of his youth, or the cowardice of modern man, and the voice would grow louder and louder until my head seemed to be vibrating, filling so forcefully with his words that for a moment, just before waking, I was unsure whether it was his voice or my own.

I'd wake with a start, my heart knocking against my chest and under clothing drenched in sweat. After such episodes, I didn't dare attempt go back to sleep the same night, and often not for several subsequent nights for fear the dream would start back up again. I'd roll out of bed, fix a pot of coffee and sit in a chair by the window looking out on the street, faintly lit by a couple of street lamps. At the window, I became familiar with creatures of the night. A marmalade alley cat would appear regularly on the curb across from my flat, loudly meowing under the streetlight. Sometimes a second, smaller, gray cat would respond and the two would go prancing down the street, thick as thieves. The craft workers of Highlandstown started and finished their shifts through the early morning hours and sometimes a bricklayer or machinist would trudge past, hands stuffed in coat pockets, head down, willing their feet forward. The night rain stirred up odors of oil and garbage from the streets and combined them with expulsions of factory exhaust to form a pungent stew that wafted through the east side of town until you could taste the city in the back of your throat.

When dawn delivered its first slivers of light, I'd begin to ready myself for work.

* * *

The print shop was a job and a paycheck, but often it felt more like a punishment than an occupation. It was owned and run methodically by a man named Ossenhoff who'd been taken in by the "new thought" movement being propelled by a growing number of self-proclaimed gurus. These gurus, who seemed to appear out of thin air, asserted that a person could attract whatever they desired merely by thinking about it in the proper fashion. If one desired great wealth (who didn't?), they needed only think themself rich, to envision it everyday with clarity and conviction and soon they'd have more money than they knew what to do with.

It was this secret universal law of attraction unknown to the poor ignorant masses (not inheritance and unchecked greed) which accounted for the wealth and fortune of men like Carnegie and Rockefeller. While these great men naturally understood and applied such principles, ordinary men like ourselves had to learn and practice them in order to taste morsels of success. These ideas rankled me to no end, and often, I found myself brooding over them, lamenting that people couldn't see the way they enabled so called "great men" to build their wealthy empires on the broken backs of "average men" who earned barely enough to survive.

Of course, I had a firsthand knowledge which now made me habitually suspicious. What was it that compelled people to place their fullest trust in men they didn't know? Blinded by their own hang ups, they couldn't see beyond their own fear and greed. Mix in a lack of faith in their own capabilities, shake and stir, and all it took was a confidence man to show up, claiming to know the way.

Ossenhoff would collect pamphlets and brochures with titles like, Thinking your way to Success, and The Five Sacred Laws of Achievement, and distribute them to us at the shop.

It was listening to him go on about the habits of great men, along with the six day work weeks, that finally spurred me to join the labor movement—an endeavor I've thrown myself into with some zeal.

One night, not long after joining the movement, I had just gotten out of a meeting sponsored by the International Pressmen's Union. The meeting had been productive and hopeful, putting me in the mood for a drink. I made my way down to a club on the Inner Harbor and was about to head in, when Kate and Harrison came walking out. We saw each other at the same time. Self-conscious and embarrassed by my prowling, I wanted to flee, but there was no avoiding them.

"Well, hello Lionel!" Kate said, sounding genuinely pleased to see me. "This is Harrison Roberts."

"A pleasure," he said, extending his chunky, upper-crust hand and taking hold of my bony, ink stained one. He kept his grip a moment longer than necessary, the way some men do to emphasize that they're honorable and men of their word. Just as I became uncomfortable, he released his grip.

"Harrison? Pleased to meet you."

He talked to me for a few minutes about "business"; as though we were old associates catching up. Business was still good for now—knock on wood—but of course in these times you could never be sure. One had to have a backup plan, eggs in more than one basket just to be safe.

While he spoke, I noticed a small smudge of black ink had transferred from my hand to the outer edge of his palm, just below the pinkie. I took a subversive satisfaction in this, thinking to myself: try as they might, the privileged can never fully clean their hands of the dirty blue collar laborer.

"Yes, that's the smart play."

"Well, I'll go fetch the Roadster and bring it around while you two catch up," he said, smiling warmly. It was a small gesture, but a gracious one which I appreciated.

"A Roadster?" I said, turning to Kate after he walked off. "You're really getting around in style these days."

"Oh, you know me, I prefer walking anyhow; I get to see more birds that way."

I'd continued to hold the feathers in my pocket—they'd become familiar and running my fingers over them soothed me. Impulsively I placed my hands in my pockets, feeling their taut smooth texture, debating whether now—presented with the chance—I should give them to her.

I'd had this vague idea of strolling into the soda shop unannounced, placing the feathers before her on the counter, explaining where they were from and what I'd been through to get them. That I realized how foolish I'd been for letting her go and the feathers were tokens of my renewed commitment, if she'd have me back. As the shop came to a complete halt, she'd walk around the counter and embrace me with tears in her eyes.

The overdone absurdity of it suddenly hit me.

"It's been quite a while, what have you been doing with yourself?" she asked.

I told her about the print shop and my recent foray into the worker's rights movement.

"That's fantastic. Something to really be proud of, Lionel."

"I'm more exhausted than proud. Between the two, there's little time for much else. What about you, how did you and Harrison meet?"

"He's a wholesaler and his family distributes all kinds of equipment for restaurants and shops, including soda machines."

"I see."

"He's a good man, a gentleman and really quite generous."

Something in me took that as a slight, though I don't believe she meant it that way.

"You look happy," I said.

"Of course I'm happy!"

The brass thump of big band music emanated out of the club. It was late and dark, and the air cold and heavy enough that I thought it might snow. She was wrapped warmly in a black fur coat buttoned to her chin that I figured he must've given her. I'd never seen it before; and it wasn't the kind of thing she would've bought for herself.

"Don't be a stranger, Lionel. You're welcome at the shop anytime," she said, purposefully holding my gaze for several seconds with a somber expression meant to keep me guessing and fretting over her intentions. Her nose was red and runny and as she took a handkerchief from her purse and wiped it,

Harrison pulled up in the Roadster and honked.

"Good to see you, Kate. Maybe I'll come by sometime, if I can ever get a moment," I said, but didn't know that I would. At sea and on the island, I realized, she'd morphed into an ideal, a distant star to see me through a turbulent voyage. Talking up close had brought back the full reality of her, all her flaws and those little things which made me cringe. In any case, it came as a relief, because whatever I'd been possessed by almost immediately loosened its grip, and my spying activities thereafter ceased.

I watched her walk to the car parked at the curb. Harrison got out, walked around and opened the door for her. A real gentleman, I thought, as they pulled out into the Saturday night traffic, then drove away down the avenue.

* * *

Bringing the Phoenix up in everyday conversation to anyone who wasn't there is a pointless chore. It rouses too many emotions, asks too many questions I can't answer, until I feel myself starting to drown. Since returning, I've avoided the ports, but recently curiosity got the better of me and I found myself snooping around the docks, asking after the ship. A dock hand I spoke with remembered it sitting idle where we'd left it for about a week, then one morning he came in to work and it was gone. I've concluded the port authorities must have confiscated it, probably towing it to one of the near shipyards to be dismantled for spare parts.

The only person from the ship I keep in touch with or speak to about it is Reynolds, and even then, it's as if we we're on our tiptoes walking through a room full of broken glass. Today, when we meet at a coffee house in West Baltimore, we get a little table outside, overlooking the street. On the other side are yellow two story row houses and a couple of tenement buildings. It's a colored neighborhood and I receive stares from passersby on the sidewalk as well as a few of the kids playing stickball in the street.

"Will you go back out to sea?" I ask him.

"If that's where I find work, then I've no choice. Well over a month we spent aboard that cursed vessel, and not a dollar to show for it."

"Just the wonderful memories. At least you've had time to brush up on your voodoo."

"Joke about it all you want, you made it home alive."

"Last week I went down to the port trying to find out what happened to the ship."

"And?"

"No one knew much of anything. I'm thinking they tugged her to one of the shipyards and put her out to pasture."

"Good riddance, if they did."

"You don't miss it just a little bit?"

Reynolds puts down his coffee cup and raises his eyebrows. "I hope the sea hasn't driven you mad, Dent."

"I'm not talking about the captain and having to look over your shoulder, worrying if you'll be shot or thrown in the brig for something you didn't do. I mean the adventure and camaraderie of it."

"Sure, there's some of that, but you can find it at your print shop or a dozen other places of employment."

"It's not the same. The shop is dark and dreary and after a few months working the presses you become like another piece of machinery. This Ossenhoff who runs the place prints out something he calls the 'Infallible Principles of Success' and has us recite them every morning like we're in bible study: 'Thou shalt perform one's duties each day with the utmost care and attention . . .' We play along to keep our jobs, but behind his back we laugh and think him a fool. I don't know—until last week I hadn't been near the port since we docked."

In the street, a tall gangly boy hits a long arcing shot over the heads of the outfielders and his teammates yell at him to hurry round the bases. We watch for a moment before Reynolds turns his attention back to me.

"You couldn't get off that ship fast enough; none of us could."

Between the spying on Kate and the captain's voice haunting my dreams, I wonder if the sea has in fact unhinged me. Reynolds seems so calm and untouched by the whole ordeal, as though it happened to someone else.

"But you must think about everything that happened; it must gnaw at you sometimes."

"What gnaws at me is not knowing when the next paycheck will come. I can survive doing handyman work for the neighbors only so long; half of them don't have anything to pay me with, anyway. More men are being let go everyday, men and women who've been at the same job for years." He pauses and his face turns opaque and introspective.

"One night," he says, "soon after we returned, I woke with a start, gasping for breath. My wife wanted to know what it was about and I decided to tell her everything—the whole A to Z of it. But a few minutes after I started talking, I stopped. I wasn't myself certain what I'd been through and it only would've scared her, given her another thing to worry over. Believe me, she has plenty to worry about already. The harder you try making sense of certain things, the more confusing they get. Better to let them drift out to sea, if you ask me."

"What if the authorities start snooping around, asking after the captain and Mathiassen?"

His face expressionless, Reynolds stares at me, letting the question hang in the air between us. "They went to the island and never returned to the ship. That's all that I know," he says.

"I guess it's all I know as well," I say, after a time.

* * *

I've begun occasionally making my way down to the docks, and after meeting with Reynolds, do precisely that. To the north, a group of trawlers and smaller, privately owned fishing boats are ported; to the south, crews are maintenancing the larger freighters, using pulleys to load and unload barrels and crates from their enormous holds. Standing at the edge of a wharf, staring at the ripples of water, I reach into my pocket and pull out the feathers. I caress them one last time, then drop them into the harbor, watching the tide pull them out until their bright colors are no longer distinguishable from the gray-blue water. The wind down here is colder and stronger and carries the salted scent of the sea. Above, gulls cry out warnings as an

osprey takes a sudden dive, fishing for its next meal. My senses
quicken and an old longing awakens. Signs of the
ocean's wildness, its untamed charm and mystery, are
all around and despite everything that's happened, I still
feel its allure.

I know now to heed the signs and if the captain
had done as much he might still be alive. I suppose I
bear an amount of responsibility for his death, and yet,
don't carry the weight of that burden. This may be in
part because I don't fully perceive him as dead; his voice
and image after all have taken up residency in both my
dreams and waking thoughts so that I don't imagine
I'll ever be entirely free of his grip. Every time, by my
own actions or words, I try to disavow his, they rise in
protest, seeming to grow stronger and more resonant.

But more so, it's because I believe he got exactly
what he deserved. Maybe the weak and dumb among
us will be weeded out, but so too will the greedy and
murderous—if they were here and able to do so,
I'm certain Mathiassen and Mr. Hugo would agree.
Sometime soon, I expect representatives from both the
Woodstock estate and police to come around asking
questions, but how will they know to look for me,
or that I even exist? And even if they are somehow
aware, how will they find me when I myself don't know
where I'll be? The anonymity of the drifter's life has its
advantages.

I've no plans at the moment to go back to sea,
but also know I won't last much longer at the print shop.
Eventually, the boss will tighten his belt and send me
packing. Or, more likely—unable to bear the staleness

and monotony—I'll heed the tide, letting it pull me forth into some new venture.

Somewhere in the Caribbean, hidden in the remote jungle of a little known island, sits an untapped goldmine. Like Reynolds, I've tried to let the memory of it dissolve at sea like the morning fog, but sometimes— my body aching after a long day at the shop, tired of the slog, of working like a dog just to barely slide by— the gold beckons to me: "You're a fool to leave me here, letting me go to waste! I'll change your meager life in ways you can't imagine!" And I think: why shouldn't I go back and claim it for myself before somebody else stumbles upon it, leaving me to wonder what might have been?

Sitting in my chair, looking out the window of my flat, I begin to scheme, musing how I might secure a ship and a benefactor to sponsor the voyage, of rounding up a crew to man the vessel. An ambition, impatient and thirsty, rises in me and I grow annoyed with the pettiness of my existence, the repetitive futility of it. Everyone and everything seem mere obstacles blocking the path to my just reward. Suddenly, I shudder and look over my shoulder, half expecting to see the captain standing behind me, hands positioned authoritatively on his hips, nodding his approval.

For a long time I remain standing there at the edge of the wharf until the force of the tide is strong enough that I widen my stance and brace myself, so as not to be swept off the pier into the harbor.

THE COMPANY
OF CROWS

Javier looked at the lunch his wife had made him, then cast a wary glance toward the crows in the vacant lot; adjacent to the garage. There were three of them in the plot of overgrown crabgrass and weeds, bordered by a low brick wall. The smaller one held a twig in its beak, puncturing holes in a closed Styrofoam sandwich container, while the two larger, louder ones stood facing the street, cawing at the intermittent traffic. His appetite had left him and he only picked at his food, rearranging the tamales and rice in the Tupperware container. He decided to try a joke he'd remembered.

"Hey boss, you hear the one about the young woman who brought her BMW in to a mechanic?"

"Don't believe I have."

"After the mechanic takes a look at the car, she asks him, 'So what's the problem?' The mechanic tells her, 'Just crap in the carburetor' and she says, 'Oh really? How often should I do that?'"

"Not bad," Eddie said, laughing silently as his shoulders and upper body jerked slightly forward.

He watched Eddie's face, searching for some give away but the eyes were impenetrable as always and after a few seconds the expression fell blank.

A year before, walking casually past the shop on his way to the post office, there had been two crows in the lot and they had spoken to him. "Look," they'd said in their screeching crow voices.

"Here is a garage and you can fix cars. Go inside and ask for a job." Of course the crows being smart birds had been right, but now he questioned himself for heeding their advice. Sure, crows were wise but not all were well intended; there were good and bad crows and he wondered if he'd been tricked. Perhaps, it was all just childish nonsense like Eddie said. At this thought he reflexively touched the seashell amulet hanging from a leather cord around his neck, caressing its ridges with his thumb and forefinger, as if apologizing for the lapse of faith.

"Business is booming my friend. Hell, at this rate I might retire early," Eddie said, running a hand through his carefully coiffed hair. He'd just finished his lunch and was seated across from Javier at a folding table beneath a canopy that extended over the paved portion of the drive. His shirt, with his name stitched above the breast pocket, was tucked neatly into his pants and his uniform traced his sturdy build with precision.

Javier understood that Eddie was a proud, image-conscious man, not only from the attention paid to grooming and physical appearance, but also from the old high school and college football trophies and photographs he kept displayed behind the counter in the customer annex. Each fall he sponsored a local Pop Warner team, helping out with uniform and equipment expenses and there were additional photographs of him posing with the teams he'd sponsored.

At times, Javier would look up from the work he was doing to see Eddie standing beyond the canopy, hands on his hips, surveying the garage and surrounding area like a lord taking a moment to admire his property holdings. The official name of the garage was "Eddie's Automotive" announced plainly on a big white sign at the bottom of the gravel drive.

"Yes, I guess we've had good luck," Javier said.

"No such thing as luck," Eddie said. "You make your own luck. And I don't want to hear about any of that superstitious twilight zone crap you're always babbling about."

Javier cringed. Eddie had made his own luck alright. "This is good. It's much better to be busy, huh boss?" he said.

A head shorter than Eddie, he was habitually hiking up the baggy blue pants that kept inching down his backside, and his singular, grease-stained work shirt which hung loosely below his waist, did not have his name on it. His hands were those of a much bigger man, strong and leathery from a life of manual labor. He'd proven himself reliable and the two men worked together amicably, although he was aware at all times of an unnamed line that should not be crossed, and was careful not say anything that might threaten Eddie's image of himself and his garage.

"Damn right it is," Eddie said.

"So maybe you can retire someplace it's not so hot."

"Yep, and I'm thinking it's finally time to put a pool in the backyard. The wife and kids have been bugging me about it for a while now. Not looking forward to dealing with the contractors and the whole mess of it."

"Hey boss, I tell you they raising our rent again?"

"Yeah, I think you mentioned it."

"I finished with the Fiat already. It's running like new."

"Good, can you have the Subaru done by four?"

"Sure, it's no problem."

Eddie glanced at his watch. "Well, it's time to get back to work."

Javier hiked up his pants and went into the bay to finish working on the Subaru.

The previous afternoon, a woman had driven up the shop's gravel and dirt drive in a light blue Mercedes convertible that coughed and jerked the entire way before conking out in front of the customer annex. Javier and Eddie had both watched from the bays, a little farther up where the hill leveled off into even ground. The woman quickly got out of the car, took three steps, stopped, looked back at the car and threw up her hands in exasperation.

"You go on ahead to lunch, I've got this," Eddie had said.

Javier washed his hands and started out of the bay. Before heading down the sloping drive, he passed Eddie and the woman outside the little customer waiting annex. "Ma'am," he was reassuring her, "I know it's a frustrating situation, but I promise we'll have it running like new in no time. Go on and help yourself to some coffee while I have a look."

But half way to the deli Javier realized he'd left his wallet in the bay and returned to the shop. As he re-entered the bay, Eddie's upper body was under the hood of the Mercedes, his arms thrashing about violently. He stopped and stepped to the side, watching as Eddie destroyed the car's timing belt and then went to work shredding the transmission. Not sure what to do, he waited until Eddie rose from under the hood, then continued quietly to the work bench and retrieved his wallet.

"Thought you went to lunch?"

Eddie had moved away from the car, ten yards from Javier, his face a red contorted ball of fury, and the coiffed hair flattened into a bird's nest. His appearance was so unfamiliar and alarming, that for a split second Javier wondered if it was not actually Eddie, but an impostor who'd entered the garage while he was out.

"I forgot my wallet."

"Yeah? Well you shouldn't go sneaking up on people like that."

"Sorry about it boss, I'll see you in a little bit."

He must know that I saw, he'd thought, but a day later it was as if nothing had happened. Eddie seemed his normal self, in good spirits even.

That first day when the crows had spoken, he'd nearly walked out during the interview.

"What's your status?" Eddie asked, after only a few questions about his experience.

"I'm not sure what you mean."

"Come on, you know. You got residency papers?"

Javier didn't answer. He'd had an impulse to flee the shop then and pretend he'd never walked in.

Eddie smiled knowingly. "Better for both of us if we keep it off the record. IRS doesn't need to know. None of their damn business anyway."

The conversation quickly veered away from the subject as Eddie went over the hours and type of help he was looking for. He'd desperately needed the job and nothing more had been said of it.

He finished with the Subaru and started on a Toyota Corolla, raising it on the lift to drain the oil, then lowering it back to the ground, putting in the new oil and cleaning out the throttle body. It was the end of his day. He went to the basin faucet in the back and scrubbed his hands under the water with the Lava soap until no more of the grease and grime would come off.

After drying his hands with a paper towel he thought of Leticia and Anna Maria and touched the seashell amulet, trying to extract from it some guidance, some sign of how to move forward. Leticia's hours had been cut at Walmart and the landlord seemed to be raising their rent every other month. Then, just a week ago, the school doctor had diagnosed Anna Maria with an asthmatic condition which made her breathing sound like a truck in need of steering fluid and an alignment. She required medication that would cost money they didn't have.

There was nothing though. No sudden clarity of vision visited him, no well-lit path appeared for him to walk down. He was tired of the moving and uncertainty, of being forever adrift. Often, he felt like a rat that couldn't show itself in the open for more than a few seconds before scurrying back down into the sewer.

He grew angry. Where had the seashell and the crows, and reading the signs ever gotten him? He could not let them stand in the way of providing for Anna Maria and Leticia. Better to be done with it. They'd become a burden and a curse. What a fool he was, believing in their power!

Business was good and Eddie would have to raise him sometime; if not this month, then the next or the one after that.

He walked out from beneath the canopy, up to the low wall of eroding bricks bordering the vacant lot, and let his finger tips caress the shell's worn familiar ridges one last time. He removed the leather cord from around his neck, and turning his head away towards the customer annex, held his hand out over the bricks, letting it fall into the unkempt grass of the lot. For a moment it seemed he could still feel the necklace in his palm, as if somehow of its own volition, it had clung to him, but when he looked, his hand was empty.

He walked the mile back to the apartment, and that evening as the three of them sat for dinner at a small table in the cramped living room, he couldn't shake his sour mood.

"I hate carrots, they're so gross," Anna Maria said after Leticia had given her a plate of fish sticks and a mixture of carrots, peas and green beans from a can.

"Have gratitude you have something at all to eat! You'll finish dinner, then do your homework," Javier snapped.

Tears welled up in the girl's big dark eyes and she spent the rest of the meal staring silently at her plate to hide the tears as she picked at her food.

As Leticia and Anna Maria cleared the table and washed the dishes, Javier remained seated at the table, a thousand miles away in a sea of self-loathing and self-pity. An hour later he was still there, staring trance like into the kitchen.

"Javier, go and talk to her instead of feeling sorry for yourself," he heard Leticia's voice, soft and low behind him. He turned in his seat to see her standing in the orange light cast by a floor lamp, noting the earnest concern in her face and the delicate beauty of her features in the dim light.

He gave a slight nod. He had known the first time he'd seen her that he would marry her. He'd been working as a construction gopher, lugging planks of wood, sheet metal and whatever else was needed around the site. In the late afternoon, through a wire mesh fence, he'd spotted her on the sidewalk, heading to the bus stop on the next block. She'd brushed her straight dark hair away from her eyes and looked up just long enough to let him know she'd noticed him. His heart had sung a song he'd never heard before, then soared until he thought he would lift off the ground and fly away.

In a few minutes he rose from the chair and went to Anna Maria's room, knocking quietly before peeking his head in the doorway. She looked up from the book she was reading at her small desk, smiled, and then went back to her book. Thumb-tacked to the wall were several drawings done in crayon and colored pencil. They were filled with stick figures and the outlines of vaguely shaped animals. In the right hand corner of each drawing was a half circle sun, emitting yellow rays.

"What are you reading?"

"It's called The Girl Who Loved Horses. I'm reading it for a book report," she said.

"It sounds very interesting. Horses are fine animals; stubborn but also strong and proud."

"Did you ever have a horse Papa?"

"Not one of my own, but I have ridden a few beautiful ones."

"I would like to have a horse some day. I would ride her across the mountains so the chupacabra couldn't get her."

Javier smiled. "The chupacabra? Where did you hear of the chupacabra?"

"We talk about them at school sometimes. They are like little vampires with fangs and they only come out at night. Irma said they killed her grandpa's chickens."

"Well, I think horses are too big for the chupacabra to harm, and if you work hard then I'm sure you will have a very nice horse some day."

"I hope so Papa."

"Good night Anna Maria."

"Good night Papa."

Gently, he closed the door and went to the kitchen. He stood looking through the kitchen window at the darkening sky and the small parking lot below. When the light no longer shone from under Anna Maria's door into the hall, he told Leticia he was stepping outside for some air. They slept in the living room and soon she would convert the futon sofa into a bed, making it up with sheets and pillows from the closet. Now she was in her chair in the corner, wearing a black shawl and knitting a blanket she'd been making for months.

"Don't be too long," she said.

Their block was lined with two-story apartment buildings and on the next block they became shops and stores. He passed the liquor store where a small group of men were huddled in the alley behind the store, then crossed Rosa Avenue, continuing by the small grocery and barber shop, both still open and doing business. He continued for three more blocks to where the street climbed steeply, and when he ascended to its highest point at a cross street, he stopped and faced south.

In the distance, the fading outline of the Tijuana hills was slowly merging with the night. He closed his eyes and concentrated, transporting himself down a series of streets and then several more miles across the border, beyond the hills spotted with shanty houses, and still farther south, to the coastal village of his ancestors. They were fisherman who'd used dinghies and rafts to pull tuna and dorado out of the sea. The discarded seashell had been a gift from his grandfather who claimed it was a token of luck, passed down for generations.

In his mind's eye, he saw his forefathers at work in their boats, and then in the evening, resting on the shore, warming their hands and eating beside a fire. He could smell the salty sea air and hear the cries of seagulls. The men, he was sure, were courageous and hardworking, but also good-natured, ready to make conversation and laugh. And always, they were honest and just. He wished he could join them on the shore to hear their stories and share the comfort of their companionship.

He had never fished as an occupation, although occasionally, when food was low, he and his friend Manuel would take their rods to the San Dieguito

River basin and try their luck. He had, in addition to the auto repair shop and construction sites, worked in many restaurants as a cook, busser, dishwasher and even a waiter. He'd done landscaping for several years, making the grass grow green and the azaleas bloom in Spring. He'd detailed cars, waxing and polishing the painted chrome until it glistened in the sun. Between regular jobs, he collected aluminum cans and any other reusable metal he could find discarded in dumpsters, trash cans or along side the road, cashing the metal in at a recycling facility for a fee.

When a job inevitably ended or the landlord raised the rent, forcing them to leave, the uprooting was undertaken with quiet efficiency. He marveled at the way Leticia and Anna Maria neatly packed their belongings without a word of complaint, as if it were simply a ritual fact of life they'd long ago resigned themselves to. But the helpless responsibility he felt for tearing them away from friends and familiar surroundings had become a weight he carried around in his chest.

When he returned, Leticia was in the converted bed and aside from a lamp on an end table, the apartment was dark.

"I wonder where you go when you're out," she said, as he undressed.

"Only to drink a bottle of tequila and gamble with the men throwing dice behind the liquor store."

Leticia allowed herself to smile slightly. "In that case you can sleep on the street with the bums and rats."

Javier pulled up the cover and laid down beside her. "Just for a walk," he said.

"It's getting late for walks."

"The air is cooler and it's quiet."

"Well, I think her condition is getting worse, this morning her breathing sounded heavy. They say it's from the pollution and smog."

"She seems okay now. Don't worry so much, we'll get her the medication."

"Did you talk to them about a raise?"

"Yes, I think it'll be soon. It's been very busy." He reached over and pulled the lamp string. "I'll talk to Eddie again."

"Good night."

"Good night."

Soon after closing his eyes, he found himself in the company of crows, a whole murder of them, silently perched upon the thick limbs of an ancient leafless tree. There were so many that the tree appeared to have sprouted enormous black leaves. Below, starting at the tree's base and extending all the way to the horizon, was the repair shop, an entire desert strewn with the rusted, skeletal remains of cars.

* * *

Javier worked on the car as Eddie tended to a pick up in the adjacent bay. The heat was unceasing and he found himself losing focus. He put on the wrong spark plugs and then was unable to properly secure the intake valves. With a towel, he wiped the sweat from his forehead and sighed. He didn't feel much like working and when they took their lunch beneath the canopy, he remained aloof and distracted as Eddie went on about the football team he'd been helping to coach. He was saying how the kids weren't being taught the proper basics and rules of the game.

"Hello, anybody home?" Eddie said, when he noticed Javier wasn't paying attention.

"I'm here," Javier said. "I was just remembering something I need to do later is all." The words came out irritable and defensive, and this caught both men off guard.

"Must be pretty important," Eddie said, regarding Javier for several seconds, and they finished their lunches in silence.

While trying to get back to work, the recollection of several customers flooded him all at once. He recalled the elderly, half-deaf Japanese man who'd brought his Toyota Avalon in for routine maintenance and stood with his mouth open as Eddie explained that the car needed a new transmission and wasn't safe to drive. Javier had driven the car into the bay and it had run well. He remembered the teacher who had gotten very upset, arguing for some time that her brakes had been just fine when she'd driven to the shop. What could have possibly happened to them since she dropped the car off? And there had been others.

"Caw caw!"

He looked up to see there were now four crows. Two of them had hopped over the bricks and were strutting about, beneath the canopy; their caws growing louder and more frequent. The newest crow's beak was misshapen, abnormally wide and a discolored orange brown. Its ancient looking feathers were ruffled and some had fallen out, exposing a naked patch of skin. He stared for a moment, dismayed both by the crows' new-found daring, and the grotesqueness of the newly-arrived bird. He turned away and when he turned back, Eddie was standing silently in the shadows of the bay entrance, looking at him. Javier shivered.

"We need to have a talk," Eddie said.

"Yes, I think we should talk."

"Well, I'll talk and you can listen."

Javier didn't move.

"I do whatever I have to, to make sure business is good. I think you understand, without business you don't have a job. We can talk about that raise if you want, but you need to keep your mouth shut." He took a step forward into the bay, peering at Javier through narrowed eyes.

"Boss, what you're doing it's wrong."

"Don't tell me about wrong. You don't even belong here. You don't exist as far as anyone that matters is concerned."

Javier reached for the seashell, remembered it was no longer around his neck, and quickly dropped his hand to his side.

"Boss, don't you see? The shop will be cursed. Even if you make money it will be no good."

"Jesus, you people never learn. You think some superstitious magic is going to save you, but it never does, and then you come running across the border, begging with your hands out. You get what you deserve."

"I never begged you. I never begged for anything. Everyday I come to work and do my job just like you."

He reached into his pocket and pulled out a key ring with keys to the bays and customer annex. As he held them out toward Eddie, they jingled in his shaking hand.

When Eddie made no move to take them, he placed the ring on the work table and began walking out. Just before he could step from the bay into the late afternoon light, Eddie moved to block his path and his head nearly bumped Eddie's chest. He felt his smallness then; felt himself being swallowed by the much larger man, and took a quick step back.

"Where you think you're going?"

The treasured domain had been threatened and he could see Eddie ready to lash out and defend it. Javier skirted around him and out of the bay. He walked until he reached the bricks, dropped to his knees, and scoured through the weeds on the other side with his hand until in a thick patch of grass abutting the bricks, he felt the leather cord. He scooped it up, placed it around his neck and continued down the drive.

"I said I'd give you a raise!" Eddie called after him.

He kept walking, saying nothing, until his pride would no longer allow him to remain silent. He stopped and turned.

"You should raise me because I did good work, because I deserve it. Not so I won't tell what you're doing," he said, aware that his legs and arms were both shaking now.

"I gave you a job!" Eddie called after him. "You say anything and I'll make sure Immigration ships your illegal ass out of the country!"

The four crows had taken to the air. They glided over the garage one at a time, then circled back, simultaneously hovering above the bays like winged shadows suspended against a deep blue sky. Javier continued down the gravel road, kicking up dust and small rocks as he walked. When he reached the

135

end of the drive, he glanced down the street: an auto dealership, a used furniture store, several restaurants, a few beauty salons.

Eddie was still atop the drive; next to the customer annex, his arms periodically rising at his sides as his voice carried down the hill. The words sailed over Javier without comprehension before dissolving in the street. Cars went past in both directions. He hiked up his pants and walked west, wearing his anonymity like an old familiar jacket.

Halfway down the block the shaking ceased and his indignation began to subside. Ahead, he could see the heat moving in soft shimmering waves and he moved toward the vision as though under a spell. At the intersection, as the walk signal blinked its invitation for him to cross, he paused and caressed the shell's familiar ridges with his fingers, awaiting the sign that would tell him he was finally home.

Troglodyte

We were in the back storage room—an enormous holding area for the countless array of items sold at Dino's Discount Warehouse. Kenny, Dombroski, and I were joking around, taking a moment's reprieve from loading and unloading boxes onto flatbeds and tubs, moving pallets and climbing ladders to stock merchandise on shelves that ascended to the ceiling rafters, high enough to give you a nose bleed. We were in a corner of the soft lines aisle, and I picked up a big cardboard box someone had left on the floor and placed it over my head.

"Hey, wait a second; I can't see! This box is trying to devour me! Help!" I called out, bumping into a cart and then a pallet jack.

"Sorry, you're on your own," Dombroski said, frowning.

"Yeah, you've worked here long enough to know about the man eating boxes," Kenny added.

"Harris!"

I removed the box and the three of us turned to see Jeff, the shipping and receiving manager, his face flushed, the veins bulging in his neck.

"Meet me in my office! Right now!"

I made my way over to Jeff's cramped little office where he commenced lecturing me about company standards, how I was pushing my luck and potential disciplinary action. He spoke of accountability and taking responsibility. It wasn't the first time we'd had this talk and it occurred to me he enjoyed them.

He'd throw in tidbits from his own past reliving lessons learned and milestones achieved. It was a stroll down memory lane for him and by the end of our talk he was reclining comfortably in his chair, smiling and twirling the hairs in his mustache. He segued into recommendations for improving work speed and efficiency. "Shipping and receiving is a thinking man's game—it's really all about planning ahead," he said.

I tried not to roll my eyes. The corporate office, driven by greed, was constantly increasing production goals and quotas with no regard for how things actually worked at the store level. Often they came up with rules and protocols that only made our work more difficult and I'd grown numb to the demands. Knowing it was useless to protest, I nodded agreeably, wondering if he actually believed the nonsense that came out of his mouth; if he woke up each morning spouting company maxims.

I strolled through the sales floor aisles back to the warehouse, self-righteously telling myself they could go ahead and fire me if my work wasn't appreciated. It was a dead-end job most people wouldn't have touched with a ten foot pole. The people they did hire usually didn't stick around for more than a few months. The ones who stayed were desperate and down and out; Dombroski was a high school drop-out who moved frequently, keeping on the down-low to avoid getting slapped with child support payments; and Kenny showed up high half the time, paranoid the managers were finally on to him. I considered myself "stuck" and think, looking back, I was daring them to fire me, secretly hoping for it. My life needed a jolt. I'd been going nowhere for some time, with neither the fortitude or know-how to change things.

I romanticized myself a suffering artist: a writer and uncompromising observer of the human condition, sitting on a mine of untapped potential. Except I'd written next to nothing. I couldn't finish a chapter without starting over—never mind a complete novel— and I actively sought out distractions. There were dishes begging to be washed, laundry to be done. I'd let myself go and needed to step outside for some exercise, which would in turn clear my mind.

I had plenty of ideas, but under closer examination they evaporated. Like short-lived clouds, the words came apart at the slightest wind. How was I supposed to ascend, to reach respectability and acclaim, when my days were being wasted stocking shelves and unloading boxes of cereal, vacuums, flat screen televisions . . .

I passed Louis pushing a tub of kitchen and cooking ware onto the floor. A huge hairy, misshapen mass of a man; his neck lurched too far forward, his shoulders were hunched and rounded, partly I presumed from lugging one too many loads around the store. He both moved and spoke slowly as if someone had hit a button that set him to half speed. A plodding earthbound creature, he rarely spoke, seeming to prefer the guttural noises of our cave-dwelling ancestors. Sounds that he made while lifting and setting boxes on pallets or just moving through his daily routine. He was a reminder of what I vowed never to let myself become: a company slave, beaten down into a shell of a man by a corporate monster devouring everything in its path.

We made fun of him—behind his back of course—calling him troglodyte, neanderthal and the like. "All these years people have been searching for Sasquatch in hidden forests and remote mountain ranges, and it turns out he's been right here among us all along, working a shit job at Dino's," Kenny quipped in a mock newscaster voice; a few days before as Dombroski and I snickered.

"Someone needs to get the guy the name of a good chiropractor," I'd added. He neither said nor did anything to indicate he was aware of our insults, but we weren't always so discreet and sometimes I suspected he knew.

When my shift was over, I went quickly out to my car in the giant parking lot. Before opening the door, I noted how the setting sun marked the sky with a purplish bruise and strained to find some metaphorical significance in it. Lately, I'd been reading Machado and other early twentieth century European poets who'd found a way to merge romantic imagery with the plight of the working man, and I stood there a minute, hoping the fiery sky would brand my soul with the hot iron of inspiration. But there was nothing—just the gurgling of my stomach still bravely attempting to digest the hot dog and chips I'd had for lunch.

The engine turned over on only the second try, putting me in a hopeful mood. There was a bus stop located just inside the plaza and as I approached, I looked through the driver's side window, unintentionally making eye contact with Louis who sat quietly on a bench beneath the stop's protective weather guard. With a slight waving gesture, he raised one of his over-sized mitts. I don't know why I stopped exactly. Maybe guilt or pity—or maybe just the surprise of someone I never would have expected, acknowledging me with a friendly gesture. Whatever the reason, I rolled down the window and heard myself ask if he needed a lift. He sat unmoving on the bench, his brow creasing above big dark eyes as if he hadn't properly understood.

"Which way you headed?"

He shrugged his shoulders and in what seemed a trick of physics, the great mass of him rose from the bench and began lumbering towards my window. Dark sweat stains were visible under the arms of his green work shirt and for the first time, I noticed he favored one leg when he walked. It wasn't quite a limp, but an acknowledgment of pain. The sight of him plodding towards me filled me with a despair that quickly turned to panic and I thought of putting the car into drive, pretending that I'd never stopped. But he was already there at the window, telling me where he lived.

We said little during the drive. He lived about fifteen minutes away—more than twice that by bus, I guessed. He advised me to turn at the intersection of Gaines and Arthur Avenue and again at a corner gas station and market. His hair grazed the sagging ceiling mesh of my old Subaru, held in by thumbtacks, and I noticed touches of gray around his temple: an unwanted reminder of the gray that had begun sprouting up in my own hair and which I quickly removed as if they were invasive weeds. He held an empty lunch container in his lap and seemed contented, but the quiet unnerved me, so I asked him about himself.

He answered in short simple sentences while looking straight ahead through the windshield. He was from the area. He had a wife and two kids. His wife worked as a secretary, but only part time, to take care of the kids.

Halfway to his place, the car, as it was wont to do, began shaking and vibrating without warning. A loud squealing noise from under the hood sounded like a rodent was trapped in the transmission.

"Looks like maybe I should've taken the bus," Louis said, grinning to let me know it was a playful barb.

"Yeah, maybe you should of," I said, annoyed. "I'd drive you back to the station, except this piece of shit probably wouldn't make it that far." There was a silence, and then we both laughed.

"See that? It got us there alright," I said, pulling into the entrance of his apartment complex. Before getting out, he nodded his round, beard-stubbled face in gratitude. I nodded back. "See you at the office," I said.

That evening in my studio apartment, I tried fleshing out a story idea I'd been toying with but could only get down a few sentences before a claustrophobic blockage set in. The tiny room seemed to be bearing down on me. A sofa stood vertical against the wall because there wasn't enough space for it. I sat at a small desk in the middle of the room, sandwiched between a mattress and the miniature kitchen from which I could glimpse the airport runway. Jets with their landing wheels clearly visible, roared directly overhead, leaving an odor of jet fuel in their wake. Several coffee mugs and glasses were on a folding table, crowded around a potted fern I'd managed to keep alive for a few years. The plant seemed to gauge me with disapproval and in one motion I rolled over onto the mattress. Closing my eyes, I imagined myself aboard one of the planes, en route to an exotic land of hidden forests and remote mountain ranges.

* * *

Our ride home didn't become a carpooling ritual, but then after when I saw him at Dino's, we'd nod at one another in acknowledgment. The following week, Kenny, Dombroski, and I were taking our break in the lot behind the warehouse. It was the usual conversation about what we would do with our lives if only we weren't stuck at Dino's, as if it were forced prison labor. The talk inevitably turned to co-workers and when Dombroski made a joke about the caveman-like noises he'd heard Louis making on the loading dock that morning, I became irritable. "Hey it's not like you don't have any strange habits," I said, before telling them I had to make a phone call and walking off.

The three of us often hung out on the weekends, cruising the town and hitting the local bars. We'd had some good times but at some point it had turned into a repetitive loop of the same places, drunken conversations and halfwit jokes. I could predict how the night would play out before it began and had recently come up with a revolving list of excuses why I couldn't join them: I was broke (very possible), I had a migraine (I'd only had a migraine once in my life), I was staying in to write (laughable).

I took up hiking: long solitary walks into the surrounding foothills and mountains. Aside from gas money it was free, and I'd gotten the notion that on one of these treks, I'd meet a beautiful disenchanted woman, also alone. Just as she'd grown skeptical of ever finding someone who understood and appreciated her, there I'd come bounding down the trail.

It was this notion which compelled me to approach a solitary woman I spotted on the trail that Saturday as the sun was beginning to set. We were walking in opposite directions: she ascending to the mountain's peak which provided a serene view of the city some twenty-five miles west, me on my way down. We were on course to meet beneath the long limber branches of several sycamore trees shading a portion of the path and as we drew closer, I thought of what I would say. She was like a mirage,   moving deftly in pink yoga pants that accentuated her lithe figure. A ponytail bounced freely beneath her baseball cap.

At ten feet, I slowed to a stop and began talking. She lowered her head in rigid determination and— taking a wide berth—stepped entirely off the path to avoid me. I should've just kept going, but instead I stopped and turned towards her, trying to explain I meant no harm and at this she pulled a pink canister of mace out of her pocket and sprayed me in the eyes. I cried out, stumbling down the path another twenty yards, kicking up clouds of dust as I went, before finally tripping over an embedded rock. I fell against one of the sycamores with my hands covering what was left of my burned-out eyes.

At some point I found the wherewithal to remove the water bottle from my backpack and wash them out, then continued down the mountain with my eyes tearing and my arms out in front of me like a blind man or sleepwalker.

I spent that night in front of the TV, anxiously switching between local newscasts to see if there'd been any reports of a hiker attack, maybe one featuring the work of a police sketch artist that resembled me. There were no such reports, but I still felt awful and not just because my eyes were still stinging. The whole ordeal felt like a referendum—a screaming alert that somewhere I'd taken an ill advised turn, that I was bumbling down the wrong path.

* * *

A week later, I received in the mail a yellow envelope with Louis' name and return address. I opened it to find a birthday invitation. "Please join us for an afternoon of food, games and fun in celebration of Louis' birthday," the card said. "We hope to see you there!" someone had written at the bottom in blue ink and I knew from the script that it wasn't Louis. I guessed he'd told his wife I'd given him a ride home and they'd decided to invite me.

Ugh, how awkward. I barely knew the guy and certainly wouldn't know anyone else there. I suspected I'd been chosen as his default work buddy since Louis didn't seem like the type who did much socializing, if any. I racked my brain for an excuse to feed him about my certain absence, settling on the lie that I'd be out of town visiting my sister and her family that weekend. In reality we'd had a falling out and hadn't spoken in years. In fact, I had almost no contact with any family.

My mother and father were both teachers and when I dropped out of college without a degree, it didn't go over well. I moved back home, declaring formal education to be a waste of time, along with my intention to become a writer while working low paying service sector jobs, and tensions rose. One evening at dinner, my father—in his stern, professorial voice— delivered the ultimatum that I would re-enroll in school, obtain a degree, and seek "respectable" employment, or move out by the end of the month. Resentful that my parents' acceptance seemed purely a condition of academic achievement, I quickly chose the latter option.

From Illinois, I drove west, and when I came for the first time upon the majestic mountain landscapes of New Mexico, Nevada and finally California, knew I wouldn't be going back.

For a period, my sister and brother would occasionally call to do my parents' bidding, condescendingly asking if I'd learned my lesson and was now ready to return home and complete my education. Insulted, I dug my heels in, eventually telling both of them in expletive filled conversations, not to contact me again.

The idea of mentioning my sister to Louis— even as part of lie concocted to avoid his party—caught me off guard. Where had that come from?

At times Louis and I would stop in the warehouse or the break room and make small talk and once he even mentioned the invitation, asking if I'd gotten it. He said it wasn't a big deal; if I couldn't make it, he understood. But I could see in his eyes that it was a big deal to him and I was unable to get the lie out of my mouth. The Saturday of the party, I tried to forget about it but couldn't seem to. The entire thing was ridiculous. No one would care if I showed up to a stupid birthday party or not and I grew annoyed that it was bothering me. So I'd given him a ride home. It didn't mean anything. I'd driven past him hundreds of times without a second thought.

Yet, here I was, pacing back and forth in the dimly lit hallway outside my apartment. I began to panic, the way I had seeing him lumber towards my car after offering him a ride. I thought of calling Kenny. He'd scored tickets to a concert that night with a band that I admired and might still have an extra ticket. At least then I'd have a legitimate excuse. But I realized how uncomfortable it would be at work. How Louis would have that wounded look whenever I saw him at the store, and in the end decided I had no choice but to make an appearance.

Before heading out, I appraised myself carefully in the bathroom mirror. I looked tired. Bags had formed under my eyes and my neck was bent slightly forward. I turned sideways. My God, was that a hunch in my upper back? I looked away in disgust and exited the bathroom, but it was too late, I'd already glimpsed my future self: a downtrodden sycophant, trudging through the aisles at Dino's, barely able to string together consecutive sentences. "Just ten minutes, in and out," I told myself.

A mousy woman with big nervous eyes, wearing dark slacks and and a white blouse, opened the door.

"Hi, I'm Connie and you must be Sam. It's so nice to finally meet you." I stepped inside the apartment. "It was kind of you to give Louis a ride home. I use the car to drive the kids around and it hasn't always been easy for him to make friends at work," she continued, as we made our way down a hallway to a living room area. So I had been chosen as the default work place buddy. Ten minutes and out, I reminded myself.

"Oh, no big deal, it wasn't too far out of the way," I said.

I'd expected at least a few other guests: relatives, in-laws, a neighbor or two, but if anyone else had shown up they were gone now. Louis was in the kitchen putting dishes away while a boy and girl, maybe ten and eight chased each other wildly around the apartment. I had no fondness for children, especially the loud hyper kind, and eyed them anxiously.

Blue and red celebratory streamers hung from the ceiling while a half-eaten orange and white cake sat on the kitchen table. The letters L and O, written in orange icing, were still intact. Louis came over to shake hands and my hand momentarily disappeared in his huge mitt. The shake seemed to go on for years. I tried to pull away, but he held on, increasing the pressure of his grip. I looked up in confusion trying to navigate his facial expression and began to perspire guiltily. Finally, he released my hand and I wondered for a moment if I'd misjudged his reason for inviting me.

"Hey there birthday boy," I said.

Dressed up, he looked odder than usual. The buttons on his collared shirt were being pushed to their limits in an effort to contain the mass of him. Connie asked if I wanted a piece of cake and the three of us sat down at the kitchen table. She did most of the talking and it fast became clear that she was in charge, and very protective of Louis. A tough little mother goose, ready to defend her flock.

"So how do you like working at Dino's?"

I shrugged. "You know, I guess it helps pay the bills."

"Louis really loves it there. Last month he celebrated his twenty year anniversary and some bigwig from corporate called us at home to congratulate him personally. Hold on." She quickly disappeared and returned with an inscribed piece of metal screwed onto a little square of wood, confirming twenty years of employment. It was cheaply put together and I imagined it coming off an assembly line with countless replicas for all the employees who had work anniversaries that month. It didn't even have his name on it.

"Twenty years? Wow, guess he really must love it," I said, glancing over at Louis. He grinned, looking both proud and a little embarrassed by Connie's excitement. He'd periodically look at her as if waiting for a cue or a directive. It was something he did at work with Jeff and the higher-ups when they came back to check on us, and had always bothered me. They didn't deserve that much deference. But now, with Connie, it wasn't so bad. There was something endearing about it.

Connie finished cleaning up in the kitchen while Louis and I moved to the big cushioned chairs in the living room. Here he was clearly at ease, in his element. His son and daughter took notice and stopped their running, seizing the opportunity to climb on him like a living, breathing jungle gym. I thought he might remove them in annoyance, send them scattering like flies, but he took great pleasure in it, lifting them high above his head with one hairy arm each, then letting them down and gently kissing them on the forehead. It was obvious they adored him and he they. I thought of my own solitary apartment and looked away ashamed, as if witnessing something I wasn't supposed to see. As I sat feigning interest in an object on the other side of the room, I felt a tap on my shoulder.

"Hi!" said the boy. "What's your name?"

"Hi, I'm Sam."

"I'm Victor. Do you work at Dino's with my dad?"

"Yes, yes I do."

"We get tons of cool stuff from Dino's. My dad gets really good discounts."

I took a moment to scan the room, then laughed at myself for failing to notice. The self-assembly book shelf and coffee table, the standing lamps, the imitation Persian rugs, pretty much all the apartment's furnishings were from Dino's.

Louis sent the kids to help his wife clean up, and when they were gone, asked if I had any hobbies.

"What, you mean like ham radio or stamp collecting? No, nothing like that," I said.

He said he had one and asked if I wanted to see it.

"Sure," I said, curious.

We walked outside, across a parking area to a row of storage sheds. He unlocked one of them and as we stood by the door, he turned to face me. He was smiling, but it was a pained smile, the kind you flashed to keep from being overwhelmed by anger or shame. He stood there looking at me without speaking until

I became uncomfortable. I could see he was doing this on purpose and wondered about his intentions, if maybe I should take off running before something bad happened—like being locked inside a shed against my will. You really don't know him that well, I warned myself. His smile disappeared and I took a step backward, watching for any sudden movements.

"I know you guys talk about me," he said.

"What?"

"At the store, you and Dombroski and Kenny. I hear you making those noises."

It was February and cold. Some large, old trees stood between the sheds and road and a gust of wind made their leafless branches bounce and sway.

"What are you talking about, Louis?"

He made a breathy noise, but this one was voluntary, full of impatience and disgust. "The other morning when we were unloading the first truck, I heard you guys on the dock laughing at Kenny making those grunting noises. Come on, admit you make fun. It's okay, I don't really mind it. I know you're not like them."

For a long moment I stood listening to the wind blow through the naked trees. "We were joking around, being stupid," I finally said, looking through the trees, out to the road. I felt trapped. I'd no idea how much time he'd spent planning this, but it was clear I'd been set up. "I mean we're grunts, we make grunting noises; we all do it."

Inside the shed, on a long table, was a sprawling miniature train track on which sat a train of six cars, each painted in meticulous, painstaking detail. In the middle of the track he'd constructed and painted a train yard with little ceramic yard workers wearing gray work hats and suspenders. The figures were carefully positioned to form a scene. Two men were carrying each side of a length of track from the yard, while a third man watched, his arm extended, pointing to where he wanted them to set the track. Two more workers were seated beside their lunch pails, facing each other in conversation. Next to the train yard, a motley assortment of passengers waited at a station. Several were standing on the platform, and a few were seated on a bench, reading. He'd cut little square pieces out of a newspaper and glued them into the figures' tiny hands.

As I marveled at the time and care it must have taken to build, he reached down to a control panel, flipped a few switches and beamed with pride as the train made its way flawlessly around the track. After a minute though, I was elsewhere, confused and stewing over our conversation outside.

* * *

Three months after his birthday party, on a warehouse ladder, retrieving an item for a customer, Louis dropped to the floor. A couple of employees walked by, saw him and called an ambulance. I'd just finished stocking bath towels on the sales floor and when I returned to the warehouse, saw him motionless, sprawled out in an aisle still clutching the item he'd retrieved: a large bag of pizza- flavored, gourmet dog treats. I stood hovering over him, searching for the slightest rise and fall of his shoulders, the trembling of a hand or foot, but there was only the unmoving mass of him blocking the aisle.

Thinking the worst, I felt myself grow unsteady like I might pass out right there next to him. I had to get out of there.

I walked off aimlessly, passing through the warehouse doors onto the sales floor. I couldn't stop thinking about the dog treats, laughing aloud at the absurdity of it. "Gourmet pizza-flavored dog treats?" I kept repeating over and over, as if unable to comprehend such a thing existed.

The aisles, already crammed with too much merchandise, were now clogged with customers pushing shopping carts and the store was a certified mess. Articles of clothing were scattered through the Toys and Games department. Someone had shoved a half empty bottle of Dr. Pepper and a crumpled bag of chips between comforters in the bedding aisle. Teenagers were playing dodge ball, using basket and soccer balls from the shelves to beam each other in the aisles. Small children screamed and had tantrums while their parents did nothing.

"Excuse me sir, do you work here? Can you tell me where to find seat covers?" a man asked. I glanced over my shoulder at him and kept walking. "Sir, excuse me!"

A loud inaudible announcement crackled over the PA system. I sensed something in me about to break, an internal damn giving way, and continued on past the checkout lines, until I was outside.

I stood absently in front of the store's big, sliding glass doors, making myself an inconvenient obstacle to the swarms of people arriving for that weekend's sale. "What's wrong with that dude?" a woman asked on her way past. A mindless, overpowering mob, obsessed with their discounts and the never-ending choices of merchandise. They may as well have been aliens. What did any of them know about us who worked in the store? What did they care if we lived or died as long as their coveted items were on the shelves? I remained there for quite some time, standing my ground like a solitary traffic cone as the the crowd flowed around me and into the store.

Louis didn't die. It turned out he'd hit his head on the floor and knocked himself unconscious. He also sprained his back and fractured a disc in his lumbar spine. An external review found the company's safety protocols weren't up to snuff and he got a hefty worker's comp settlement out of it. Almost immediately after the payout, he and the family moved to Florida.
Louis survived, but my initial reaction to his fall couldn't be undone or simply erased from memory. Seeing him sprawled on the warehouse floor changed something in me, sent me hurtling in a new
direction.

At first I was embarrassed by it, careful not to tell Kenny or Dombroski about my new-found ambition. I knew what their reactions would be and after spending years complaining and badmouthing Dino's, I felt like a sellout. To be honest, after my run-ins with Jeff, I didn't think I'd
actually get the shift manager position.

When he called me into his office, I figured it was for some task I'd forgotten, an overdue training or clerical requirement. He started in on one of his long winded speeches, talking about accountability, "owning one's mistakes and foolish indiscretions," as he put it, and I thought I was being fired. I was trying to remember how to file for unemployment when again his tone changed as he recalled with nostalgia one of his own youthful mistakes, something to do with dating a direct subordinate on the down low, and how everyone deserved a second chance. A half hour passed before I realized what he was trying to tell me.

"I've always thought you had managerial potential, Harris."

"Really?"

"Yeah, I mean it's not obvious to the untrained eye. You have to look beneath the baggage and maturity issues to find it, but it's there."

It happened fast, deciding I couldn't spend the rest of my life in that cramped apartment inhaling jet fuel exhaust, driving a car where the next trip might be a tow to the junk heap. As soon as they found out, Dombroski and Kenny started giving me the cold shoulder.

"Dombroski, where's your name badge?" I said, testing my newly claimed authority as I passed him in Electronics one morning.

"That's quite a power trip you're on, Harris. You must feel like a real big man now," he said, sneering.

"Dombroski, come here a second," I called after him as he walked away, but he wouldn't turn around.

When it happened a second time and he told me off again, I wrote him up for insubordination which led to his firing. I know it sounds petty, reprimanding employees for name tag violations, or because they refer to a shopper as a "customer" rather than a "guest," but when I took the supervisor position I knew if I didn't go all in, I wouldn't last long. Maybe I went too far in the other direction, but I figure if you're going to take a job, then you should actually do it, otherwise what's the point? Sometimes I alarm myself, barking at the guys in the warehouse to follow safety protocols when climbing ladders or using the electric lift. The old me would've rolled my eyes and cursed such instruction, but honestly, the old me was a chronic complainer and slacker. All the criticizing of management and the company for not being perfect—at some point it just becomes an excuse not to aspire: a sort of cowardly hiding in plain view.

The same week Dombroski got fired, Kenny and I were in our cars, pulling out of the plaza parking lot at the same time. When I looked over at him, he flipped me the bird. Later that week, he stopped showing up. Monday, the following week, I walked out to my Subaru to find the tires slashed. Someone had written the word, "Tool," in red spray paint across the driver's side door. It didn't require a detective's license to figure out who was responsible. For a minute I was furious. I kicked one of the flattened tires, cursing and threatening to file a police report. A guy with a shaved head and grizzled beard had just parked. Hearing me making a fuss, he came over to survey the damage. "Damn boss, you must've really pissed someone off," he said.

After cooling off a bit I decided no, I wouldn't file a complaint. With my significant pay hike, I already planned to buy a new car which I could now afford to make payments on, and it wasn't like that piece of junk was worth anything anyway. In my head I resolved the situation this way: Dombroski, Kenny and I were even. I was responsible, to a certain extent, for them losing their jobs and I suppose in some contorted way I'd sold our friendship out for greener pastures. Nothing pisses the apathetic off more than an act of ambition. Now they'd gotten me back; if they tried anything else, all bets were off. As it happened, Dombroski soon had

greater forces to contend with— last I heard, child support
services tracked him down and he'd done a stint in the
county jail for non-payment.

Now I'm the one enforcing the quotas and
production goals from corporate. I know the employees
working under me talk about me the way I used to
talk about Jeff, but so what? Why worry about what
other people think? They don't know what you've been
through, what you've seen.

I don't miss climbing those nose-bleed ladders
or lugging around flatbeds loaded with merchandise.
I walk the aisles, checking inventory on the shelves or
catch up on paperwork in my office. I drive to work
in my new car, a used Lexus with an engine so quiet,
sometimes when I'm stopped at a light I turn down the
stereo and lower my head to make sure it's running.

On my days off, I zip around town with no
particular destination, content knowing that wherever
I decide, I'll get there without a problem. Often, I
drive out to the bay. I park in the shade, close to the
pedestrian path and sit in my car waiting for the sun
to go down. I don't waste time waiting for a state of
transcendent artistic bliss that probably doesn't even
exist. I just roll down the windows and watch the
women running, biking, walking their dogs. Listening to
their headphones, talking on their earbuds—they move
fast, going somewhere important. Sometimes I'll get a
look of curiosity or a sideways glance—I think it's the
car that gets their attention. It sure doesn't hurt; that old
eyesore I used to clunk around in would've sent them
scattering in the opposite direction, reaching for their
mace.

A Long Night
at the
Grab N' Go

It was late and the Grab N' Go was empty now. No one had come into the store for several minutes and the two young men working the night shift stood behind the counter talking, passing the time.

"Ten more minutes and I'm out of jail," said the older one.

"Jail?" the younger one, replied. He was nineteen, of medium height and build with a full head of curly brown hair. His pleasant, unassuming face and open disposition endeared him to some of the oddballs, vagrants and insomniacs who wandered into the store at this hour.

"You heard me right. This is no place to be on a Saturday night."

"I don't mind it; I think it gets kind of interesting sometimes," said the younger man, looking through the big pane glass window. Outside, the entrance walkway was illuminated by the orange glow of a lamppost and the neon from the sign above the store. Beyond the walkway was a parking lot littered with food wrappers, flattened paper coffee cups and cigarette butts. Beyond that, a two lane residential road traveled at a slight incline for a quarter of mile until it met the avenue.

"That's because you don't have anything better to do," said his co-worker who was taller, three years older and had begun to develop a gut protruding over his belt. "You don't have a girl. My girl's already texted me three times asking when I can get out of here."

"What're you guys going to do tonight?"

The co-worker shrugged. "Probably cruise the avenue and see what's going on, maybe stop by Henry's Tavern. Doesn't matter as long as it isn't here. Can you handle the store by yourself for a few hours?"

"Yeah, no problem."

"You sure?"

"Yeah, I'm sure," he said again.

"What if gangbangers come in and rob the place? It happens all the time."

The younger man, whose name was Gabriel, smirked and shook his head. He didn't believe Ricky. The previous week when he didn't think anyone was watching, Gabriel saw him take a twenty out of the register and slip it into his pocket.

"It only happened once and that was just some homeless guy with a screwdriver."

"No, it happened a few times before you worked here, guys holding the place up at gun point."

"Are you sure?" Gabriel asked. Surprise and fear contorted his normally placid face as though he'd tasted something rotten. Gerry, the owner, hadn't mentioned anything like that.

"Yeah, for real. So what would you do if it happened?"

"Well, you're supposed to do what they say. Give em' the money, it's not worth getting shot over."

Ricky smiled cleverly at Gabriel's answer. "That's it? I thought you wanted to join the police. You'd let those punks just stroll out of here? 'Hey, would you guys like a bag to carry the cash in?'"

"What would you do?" Gabriel asked, irritated.

Ricky checked his watch. "I'll tell you later, right now it's time to clock out."

"Alright, have a good night Ricky."

"You too, be safe."

Gabriel had only worked the graveyard shift by himself twice before, and then there'd been enough traffic in the store that he didn't have time to think about anything else. Now, with the store empty, he thought about his conversation with Ricky, bothered by how it had gone, how it made him look weak and afraid. "He's lying through his teeth," he told himself. "Anyways, I wouldn't let them walk out easy; those thugs would have a fight on their hands."

But what was he supposed to do if they pointed a gun? He could grab it before they knew what was happening and wrestle it away, or he'd talk them out of it, convincing them that robbing the store just wasn't worth it, that they'd end up in prison, their lives ruined. The story would be all over the papers and TV news, how he'd shown these wayward criminals the light, convincing them to change their ways. Afterwards, he would be put in charge, given full authority to run the store as he saw fit. "I'm sorry," he'd say when Ricky came into work twenty minutes late. "After a thorough review, I've decided you're too dumb and irresponsible to work here any longer. Your dishonesty is hurting the business. No, I've made my decision. Stop begging, Ricky; it's embarassing."

Pleased by how the situation had resolved in his reverie, he grinned and let out an audible breath. With still no customers, the sounds of the store occupied his attention. The ice machine against the wall, facing the counter, rumbled and churned and spat ice into the bin. The refrigerated shelves holding sodas, sports drinks, energy drinks, and beer, hummed, while above, the white fluorescent ceiling lights produced a hypnotic buzz. Taking advantage of the down time, he fetched a wet mop from the closet and moved it back and forth across the floor in front of the counter in slow, even motions, cleaning away the footprints and muck that had accumulated. After mopping, he got a broom and dustpan, went outside and swept the front walkway.

The night air was refreshingly cool and he thought he could hear the faint sound of traffic coming from the avenue. It seemed a world away. As he swept, he heard a rustling noise come from the side of the store by the dumpster, then stop. Holding the broom still, he squinted through the darkness, listening carefully. There it was again. Still holding the broom, he began walking towards the noise. Just as he reached the end of the walkway and stepped into the parking lot, a bearded man popped his head out of the dumpster.

"Jesus, Rhodes, you scared the hell out of me."

"Looking for Lucky Charms."

"Lucky Charms?"

"Yeah, a few days ago I found a whole box of em', one of those family size boxes, unopened. I finally realized it's true."

"You realized what's true?" Gabriel leaned towards Rhodes as though he were about to reveal some profound piece of wisdom.

"The goddamned things really are magically delicious."

"I've got a few hoagies that are about to expire if you're hungry."

Rhodes shrugged with indifference, dropped the torn, rain sogged bag of half eaten fast food he was holding and climbed out of the dumpster.

Gabriel was glad to see him, glad not to be by himself. Sometimes Rhodes smelled really bad from sleeping in a self-made hovel next to the river and hours spent digging through dumpsters for discarded goods which he referred to as "treasure hunting," but Gabriel found him harmless and his stories were always entertaining. There was something exciting, even romantic, about his life of daily survival on society's fringe. Just before they got to the door, Rhodes stopped and looked back, scouring the parking lot and road. "Have they been around already?"

"Huh? Oh, you mean the police? No, not yet. They don't stop in until after eleven thirty." Gabriel checked his watch. "It's only ten past, I wouldn't worry about it Rhodes." he said, hoping he wouldn't leave.

"Yeah, that's because they ain't looking for you," Rhodes said, turning to give Gabriel a stern look. He turned back to scour the area again and when he was satisfied, followed Gabriel into the store.

Gabriel gave him one of the expired hoagies he'd removed from the shelf and with his own money

Rhodes bought a thirty two ounce can of beer, a key ring and candy bar. They stood at the register for a few minutes as Rhodes talked about how a stray dog by the river he'd been working on for months had finally eaten a piece of beef jerky out of his hand.

A car went by on the residential side road and Gabriel looked up. "Looks like the officer is a little early tonight."

"What? Was that him?" Rhodes turned from the counter and faced the road.

"Yeah, first he checks on the gas station down the street. Should be here in a few minutes."

"Mother . . ." Rhodes snatched the bag of items off the counter and hurried out the door.
Gabriel watched, expecting he'd grab his grocery cart parked beside the dumpster and move along. Instead, he pushed the cart overflowing with old fraying blankets and recyclables out of sight behind the dumpster, then climbed right back in. A few minutes later, Officer Billings pulled into the lot.

"Everything good?" he said, knocking on the counter with his knuckles as he passed by Gabriel.

"Good evening, officer. No problems here."

"That's what I like to hear," Billings said, nodding.

After a cursory walk through the store, he approached the register. "Gabriel," he said slowly, as his eyes dropped to chest level. Gabriel looked down self consciously at the name tag pinned to his blue work vest. Below his name, the words, "How can I help you," were inscribed.

"Gabriel, my shift's about to end and I'd like a couple of pepperoni pizzas. Can you throw a couple of those in for me?"

Something moved outside and his attention floated past the officer, through the pane glass window. He saw Rhodes' head peering over the top of the dumpster, then quickly disappear.

"Two pepperoni, I'm already on it." He bent down, took two pizzas out of the freezer, unwrapped them, set the timers on each of the counter top ovens and put them in.

"It's been a long night," Billings said. The outline of his close cropped hair formed a V shape on his forehead and was graying at the temples. His large arms and chest appeared comically over developed set atop his thin legs.

"Thanks for keeping the peace, sir. I bet there's never a dull moment."

"You said it."

"I'm actually thinking of joining the police force, myself."

"Is that right? I know for a fact we're hiring, but you better be ready to deal with the crazies. These nut jobs living on the streets are everywhere and they're multiplying faster than flies. Too many flies and not enough fly swatters. You know how to use a fly swatter, Gabriel?" he said, grinning.

"Yeah, for sure. I've used them before," Gabriel said, squinting in confusion.

"They're capable of anything. I mean they got nothin' to lose so what do they care? Did you graduate high school?"

"Yes sir, a couple of years ago."

"Any kind of criminal record? Petty theft, underage drinking, drug possession?"

"No, nothing like that."

169

"Well that's a good start. Those are the first questions they're gonna ask you. Why do you want to get into law enforcement?"

"Well, I—"

Officer Billings held up one hand like he was halting traffic at the scene of accident and with the other pulled a cellphone out of his pocket and held it against his ear. "Yeah? I thought you might like that . . ." He walked out the door, continuing his conversation on the walkway in front of the window.

Gabriel leaned against the counter watching him pace back and forth. At one point, he stopped pacing, gestured in the air with his hand and laughed. Gabriel craned his neck and peered toward the dumpster, hoping Rhodes wouldn't pop his head out again. He hated to think what would happen if the officer caught him in there. Rhodes wasn't one to follow orders and if he disobeyed the officer might use his billy club. If someone disobeyed, were the police allowed to bash them with the club? He guessed that they could.

* * *

He wanted to be a police officer, but he also wanted to be a professional baseball player, a locksmith, movie actor and astronaut. He lived a five minute drive from the store in a small three bedroom row house with his mother, step-father, sister, and grandmother. It was his step-father's idea that he become a policeman. Nearly every evening, after his third or fourth beer, watching television, he'd tell Gabriel how the world had gone to hell: "The scoundrels are completely shameless. They don't want to work. They get their welfare checks and when that runs out they rob and steal and sell drugs to little kids, tell em' it's candy so the kids will get addicted. It's a horrible situation and no one does anything. These cartel members come across the border in broad daylight and no one blinks. You could help put an end to it, buddy, put those scoundrels behind bars where they belong."

His step-father hadn't held a job since he'd moved in with them; he claimed to have a herniated disc and bunions on his feet which prevented him doing manual labor, though he sometimes mowed the lawn and Gabriel had never seen him in pain or walking gingerly. The police had been called to the residence more than once when—after countless beers—his step-father had argued so loudly with his mother, someone had called in a complaint. She would've already left him but she depended on the government check he received each month to pay the mortgage. The irony of his step-father's evening rants wasn't completely lost on him, but neither did he think much about it.

The more he entertained the idea of working for the police, the more enticing it became. His favorite movie was the police drama Fields of Honor," which he'd watched countless times, often imagining himself in the roles of the heroic officers, reciting the lines by heart. His mother agreed that "Officer Sterling" had a nice ring to it, while at meals his sister playfully teased him, speaking in a distressed damsel voice: "Oh Officer, the salt and pepper have gone missing, please help."

The police had last been called to the house three weeks before. The following day he'd been sitting at the kitchen table talking to his grandmother, a retired garment worker and seamstress. When she wasn't stitching together a sweater or blouse for someone, she liked to drink coffee and sit on the front porch smoking Camel cigarettes, reading her celebrity gossip magazines.

"I thought they'd take him away this time," she said, standing at the counter sink, waiting for her coffee to brew. "I wouldn't've called if I'd known they wouldn't do anything." Her voice sounded low and far away and she looked like someone had stolen her prized sewing machine.

Gabriel thought about what she was saying. "It was you who called them, Grams?"

"Hell yes it was me. I'm sick of listening to him, sick of looking at his weaselly face."

That had been a revelation; he'd always assumed it was the neighbors making the complaints. Not sure how to feel about it, he dropped his head and stared silently at the kitchen table.

Having the cops at the house in the middle of night brought people out of their homes. Standing on the porch while the police spoke with his mother and step-father—who were still barking at each other from opposite ends of the lawn—he could see them all the way down the block, porch lights turning on as they came outside to watch and gossip about the screwed up family down the street. It was worse than embarrassing; a stain he suspected he'd carry around for a long time after. And yet, he couldn't really blame Grams. It wasn't her fault they wouldn't let her sleep and read her magazines in peace.

* * *

The timers sounded and Gabriel used the aluminum peel to remove the pizzas from the ovens, placed them in boxes, and sliced them into eighths.

A few minutes later, Billings re-entered the store and Gabriel stacked the warm pizzas boxes on the counter.

"Alright, that'll be twenty-three fifty, sir."

"Hey, I've been on this beat for a while, you've seen me before, right?" Officer Billings said, making no move to reach for his wallet.

"Sure, I remember you," Gabriel said, frowning in puzzlement.

"I keep a close eye on the place, make sure you guys are safe," Billings said, and an earnest grin reached across his wide, square jawed face. He took a step toward the pizzas on the counter, still not reaching for his wallet and Gabriel started to understand .

"We really appreciate what you do, keeping tabs on us over here."

"We good?" Billings said, picking up the boxes.

"Of course. On the house, officer," he said, waving his hand.

"Appreciate it, Gabriel."

"Coast is clear, you can come up for air," Gabriel said, standing outside, beside the dumpster. A few seconds later Rhodes appeared wearing a soiled safari hat with a big hole in the brim. "How do you like the new helmet?" he asked.

"It's got a hole in it, Rhodes, and it's kind of dirty."

"Well they wouldn't've thrown it away if it was brand new. Don't be so picky."

He watched as Rhodes took hold of the edge of the dumpster with both hands and pulled himself over the side. When his feet were securely on the pavement, he craned his long neck and stuck his red swollen nose in the air like a dog trying to catch a scent and re-claim a lost trail. He wore sagging green pants held up by a piece of rope tied around the waist. His old shoes were caked with dirt and the rubber soles had detached from the rest of the shoe, creating gaps through which Gabriel could see his blistered feet. Fastened to his rope belt was a little stuffed animal, a smiling turtle he called "Mr. Green."

Rhodes straightened his new hat. "That cop ask about me?" he wanted know.

"It's like you were never here."

"Luckily I have a strong ghost mode."

"What's that, some kind of superpower?"

"It's when you turn invisible so only people you want to see you can see you."

"That's impossible, Rhodes."

"Oh yeah? What the hell do you know about it, anyway?"

"Alright, then show me how you do it. Teach me ghost mode," Gabriel said, trying to contain his grin.

Rhodes' expression grew pensive as his gaze traveled across the lot to the darkened street. "I can't teach you right now. It takes years of practice to develop and most people still never get it," he said.

"Well, it sounds like a cool trick. It sure would come in handy," Gabriel said, his gaze following Rhodes' down the street.

"Here, hold on a second." He brought the cart out from behind the dumpster then reached into it, searching with his hand beneath the recyclables and blankets. Soon, he pulled out a medallion, a plastic imitation embroidered with an eagle, and handed it to Gabriel. "It'll help your ghost mode."

"Thanks, Rhodes." He put the pendant in his pocket and remained outside for a minute, watching

Rhodes rattle his cart across the lot while Mr. Green bounced gently against his hip.

A Prius pulled into the lot and Gabriel went back inside the store. It was a ride-share driver, a middle-aged Arabic man. He bought a coffee, a blueberry muffin and a package of auto air fresheners. Gabriel rang him up and as he was watching the Prius pull out of the lot, he noticed police lights flashing down the road. Curious, he stepped outside onto the front walkway, then down the step and further out into the parking lot.

A block away, just before the gas station, Rhodes' shopping cart was lying in the street, his blankets and recyclables strewn over the road and curb. There were two police cars and Rhodes was yelling at Officer Billings and another policeman attempting to restrain him. He wanted to know what Rhodes was so upset about but was only able to catch intermittent words and phrases. He heard: "Army of Darkness," "universe," "fish heads," and ". . . your little jailbird."

The two officers wrestled him to the ground, face down on the grass between the curb and sidewalk. Gabriel was worried they'd use their clubs and he wanted to tell them Rhodes was okay, that he wasn't a dangerous criminal. Maybe they would listen and let him go. He started walking across the parking lot towards the road but after a few steps, stopped. He wasn't supposed to leave the store and if Gerry found out he might get fired.

They had Rhodes restrained; his arms and ankles hogtied behind his back. He watched for another moment as they picked him up and placed him in the back seat of one of the cars.

Inside the store, he stopped on the customer side of the counter, placed both hands on it, and bent his head down between his shoulders. "'I keep an eye on you guys'; yeah sure you do," he said, bitterly. Next time, he wouldn't fall for it—he'd make the thief Billings pay like everyone else.

* * *

On the register side of the counter he stared at his watch. It was only twenty past midnight; almost another two hours before his shift ended, and suddenly, he felt unsure whether he would make it. He thought of taking his work vest off, leaving it on the counter and walking out. A few customers came in and after ringing them up, knew he wouldn't quit—he didn't want Drew to think he was scared, or that he couldn't handle the store by himself—but he still felt sick about Rhodes, wishing he'd done something to help him. He didn't care about about becoming a policeman or actor; he only wanted to make it through his shift, go home and crawl into bed.

He turned his attention back to the store's parade of sounds: the rumbling and churning of the ice machine followed by the refrigerator's hum and the buzzing of the lights. When he looked again at the watch, the minute hand appeared to be in the same place. How? Was it broken? He couldn't seem to remember a time before he'd worked at the store, or see ahead to a future beyond it.

He wondered what would happen to Rhodes; if he was really "crazy" like Billings said. He didn't seem crazy, at least not in a dangerous way. Rhodes was always friendly with him. He wondered if his mother had remembered to leave the porch light on; if she'd made him a dinner plate and put it in the fridge. These things now seemed of great importance, as though their existence would ensure his safe arrival home.

The two a.m. shift was worked by a persistently affable, middle aged man, named Carl who juggled three jobs to support his wife and children. When a car pulled into the parking lot at a quarter to two, Gabriel assumed it was Carl arriving early for his shift, but quickly realized it was not his car. Carl drove a minivan and this was a dark sedan, an Impala maybe, with tinted windows that hovered for a moment just inside the parking lot entrance, then continued towards the store at a crawl. It's headlights flooded the glass with a glare, causing Gabriel to raise his arm in front of his eyes. Seconds later, the headlights went dark and the car had taken a spot in the shadows, barely visible through the window to Gabriel's left, its engine idling.

Minutes passed and no one opened a door or cracked a window. Gabriel's palms were sweating. He placed his hands absently under the counter, then wiped them on his pants. Where was Carl? Didn't he normally arrive early? The store attracted all kinds of weirdos and shady elements at this hour, but something about this car— the way it had cautiously entered the lot as though someone inside was sizing up the store, intentionally parking just out of view of the window— felt different. He sensed something strategic and sinister at work.

The driver's door opened. A lanky man wearing baggy pants and a dark hoodie got out and shut the door. The oversized hood was purposefully drawn over his face, hiding features already shrouded by night. A second man, short and stocky, opened the passenger side door. He also wore a hoodie and sweatpants. By the car's front tire, they conferred for a few seconds then made their way up to the entrance walkway. Gabriel tried to swallow but his throat was too dry and instead, made a clicking noise with his tongue against the roof of his mouth. He'd never been so thirsty. He looked past the parking lot to the road impatiently hoping someone else would drive up and come into the store. Maybe Ms. Simon, an elderly woman who used a walker and talked with a deep rasp, would stop in to buy her lottery ticket and peach Schnapps. Maybe one of the vendor trucks that restocked the soft drinks and beer overnight, would arrive—someone.

Again, the two men stopped to confer—this time right in front of the door. "Stay out here and watch the door in case they come," he heard the lanky one say.

Gabriel looked again at the road, this time trying with his mind to will a vehicle into sight, and miraculously in the very next moment, the yellow glow of headlights were visible. A few seconds later, a pickup truck came into view and he let out a heavy breath. But the truck barreled past without slowing, disappearing as quickly as it had appeared, leaving Gabriel to watch the tail lights fade as it made its way up the incline toward the avenue.

The man opened the door, entering the store with his head down, while Gabriel stood unmoving behind the counter, waiting. One of thte man's hands was jammed inside his baggy pants, appearing to hold an object against his leg or hip. What else could it be? Gabriel thought, wishing there really was a ghost mode; that it wasn't jut some crazy idea concocted by Rhodes to put his mind at ease. He wished he'd taken off the vest and walked out when he had the chance. He strained to quickly think of something to do, but what came to him were images of his mother, Grams, and his sister, their faces as real and vivid as though they were standing right beside him. The man was at the counter now and when he looked up, a pair of large dark eyes stared out at him from inside the hoodie. He tried to read them, to infer from them some intent, but they were vacant, impassive orbs.

"Alright, Gabriel," the man said, lowering his gaze. "It's been a long night; let's make this quick."

Printed in the USA
CPSIA information can be obtained
at www.ICGtesting.com
LVHW010615280124
769814LV00075B/2680

9 798218 343248